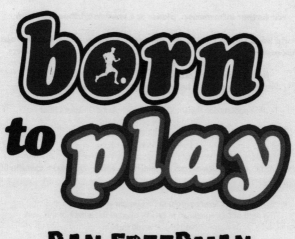

born to play

DAN FREEDMAN

NATIONAL BOOK tokens

This book has been specially written and published for World Book Day 2010.

World Book Day is a worldwide celebration of books and reading, with events held last year in countries as far apart as Afghanistan and Australia, Nigeria and Uruguay.

For further information, please see www.worldbookday.com

World Book Day in the UK and Ireland is made possible by generous sponsorship from National Book Tokens, participating publishers, authors and booksellers.
Booksellers who accept the £1 World Book Day Token kindly agree to bear the full cost of redeeming it.

First published in the UK in 2010 by Scholastic Children's Books
An imprint of Scholastic Ltd
Euston House, 24 Eversholt Street
London, NW1 1DB, UK
Registered office: Westfield Road, Southam, Warwickshire, CV47 0RA
SCHOLASTIC and associated logos are trademarks and/or registered trademarks of Scholastic Inc.

Text copyright © Dan Freedman, 2010
The right of Dan Freedman to be identified as the author of this work has been asserted by him.

ISBN 978 0956 28777 9

A CIP catalogue record for this book is available from the British Library.

Papers used by Scholastic Children's Books
are made from wood grown in sustainable forests.

1 3 5 7 9 10 8 6 4 2

www.scholastic.co.uk/zone

Over His Head

Thursday 14 October

The ball was in the air.

Jamie had his back to the goal.

He knew he had to try it.

If he pulled it off, if he scored with an overhead kick in front of everyone in the playground, Jamie Johnson knew it would be one of the best moments of his life.

It would shut up Bryn Staunton and Tyler Forbes for days and it would prove, once and for all, that he was easily the best player in the whole of Year Seven.

Although he had all the other skills, Jamie had never done a proper overhead kick before – but he knew he had to go for it. Now.

Jamie kept his eye on the ball as it seemed to hover above his shoulder. Then he launched his body into the air to meet it.

Jamie flew high above the hard cement of the playground, his body soaring towards its target.

In the air, Jamie snapped his legs back over his head in a scissors-like motion, just as he'd seen the best players do on TV.

He closed his eyes and waited for the contact with the ball. He wanted to hammer it home. He waited and hoped for the sweet sensation of the perfect strike.

But it didn't come. He felt his left foot barely scuff the side of the ball, slicing it sideways. And now, gravity played its part, dragging Jamie back down to earth with alarming speed.

Jamie crashed back down on to the gravel with a loud, wet, painful thud.

His mind screamed with anger, while his body stung with the pain. The entire layer of skin on Jamie's kneecap had been scraped off.

The blood from his gravel-filled knee started to spill through the hole in his trousers.

Jamie Johnson was going to be a big star one day. He just knew it. He wanted to be a professional footballer when he grew up. And not just any old professional footballer. He wanted to be the best. He wanted everyone in the world to know who Jamie Johnson was. And sometimes, if he closed his eyes and concentrated hard enough, he could already imagine the fans singing his name:

One Jamie Johnson. . . There's only one Jamie Johnson. . .

But that was not the song that the other boys were singing in the playground today.

Instead, as Jamie wiped his dirty, wet hands down his bloodied trousers, Bryn Staunton and Tyler Forbes were singing:

"He's small, he's thick, he can't do overhead kicks! He's Jamie Johnson, Jamie Johnson. . ."

This was easily the second most embarrassing moment of Jamie's life. The only time that beat it was the day when, at his primary school, Wheatlands, he had wet himself at the end of assembly – in front of the whole school. That was horrendous, but this wasn't far behind; Jamie didn't mind looking like a fool in lessons or people taking the mickey out of him for wearing old clothes. But he never thought the day would come where people would tease him about how he played football.

He wanted people to think of him as a football genius. But right now, he looked like a football chump.

These matches at break-time were the most

important part of the day for all the footballers at school. If you were on the winning side, you were king for the rest of the day. If you lost, you knew you wouldn't be allowed to forget it.

Bryn Staunton and Tyler Forbes – the two biggest boys in Jamie's year – always made sure that they were on the same side in break and they never picked Jamie. Ever.

It wasn't because he wasn't good enough; in fact, it was the exact opposite. It was *because* Jamie was the best player in the whole year that they had it in for him.

"Forget about them," said Hugo Bogson, the only real friend that Jamie had made at The Grove so far, helping Jamie up. "They're idiots."

"Thanks," said Jamie, carefully avoiding Hugo's outstretched hand, which was filthy.

They were mates and Jamie appreciated Hugo sticking up for him, but he also knew that Hugo was one of the dirtiest people he'd ever met. Jamie always tried not to touch him directly.

Still, no matter how weird Hugo Bogson was, he wasn't ever horrible to other kids in the way that Bryn and Tyler were. In fact, Jamie had never seen Hugo be mean to anyone, and that's what Jamie liked about him.

2

Wish List

It took Jamie ages to get home from school. He missed the bus and had to stand waiting in the rain for twenty minutes for the next one to come. He was drenched to the bone by the time he got in.

Some of the other kids called their mums and got lifts home, but Jamie couldn't do that. His mum was on a late shift at the hospital. She wouldn't be home until ten. And anyway, even if she was home, she couldn't have given him a lift. Her car was broken. It had just been sitting uselessly in the drive for the last six months and now it was going to cost way too much to fix.

Sometimes Jamie felt sorry for his mum. It was a

horrible feeling to have. He knew you shouldn't feel sorry for your parents.

Jamie wondered how he would feel if his mum got married again. Loads of the kids at school hated their stepdads. But Jamie wouldn't mind. He just wanted his mum to be happy. If she wanted to get married again, that would be fine by Jamie – as long as the bloke was a Hawkstone United fan! That would be his only demand!

Jamie put the chicken and noodles his mum had left him into the microwave and turned it on to full power. Then he checked the time: 8.18 p.m. His granddad, Mike, would be over soon to check he was OK. He always did that when Jamie's mum was working. It was cool; they just watched TV together and Mike let Jamie watch whatever he wanted!

In a way, it was good that Jamie's mum wasn't home. If she had been, Jamie would have had to explain the state his trousers were in and then his mum would have got angry about buying a new pair.

"We're not exactly rolling in it, Jamie!" he could imagine her saying.

While his dinner was cooking, Jamie ripped a piece of paper from the pad next to the phone and sat down on a stool in the kitchen. He began to write down his wish list of things that he wanted to happen in his life:

JAMIE JOHNSON – 10 THINGS I WANT
(Written on October 14 – aged 11 & a third)

1 To do proper overhead kicks!

2 To be rich when I'm older!!

3 New shinpads (mine are finished, every kick kills my shins!)

4 A younger brother so I can teach him football and other stuff

5 To buy a new car for Mum

~~6 Kiss J~~

6 To learn Tae kwon do off Jack so no one messes with me!!

7 To have big muscles (including a six-pack)!!

8 To be really famous so everyone knows me

9 TO BE A PROFESSIONAL FOOTBALLER!!!!!

The ping of the microwave went before Jamie had written down number ten.

He'd fill that one in another time. Plus, if he could achieve number nine, then nothing else would matter anyway!

If he became a professional footballer, Jamie Johnson could have everything he wanted.

That night, as he got into bed and turned out his light, Jamie's mood darkened. He'd had a good evening with Mike but now, just as he wanted to get to sleep, he began to feel unsettled. His thoughts and worries were swimming like evil sharks around his mind.

He tried to fend them off by focusing on good things, like football. He asked himself questions: how much money would his favourite team, Hawkstone United, spend in the next transfer window? What would his top world XI be?

Normally football kept the bad feelings away. But tonight it was no good. The negative thoughts were taking over his brain. . .

Why did his life have to be so hard? Why couldn't he have a nice easy life like the other kids?

Two parents and a car that worked – was that too much to ask for?!

Jamie didn't want to go to school the next day. He didn't want to be the butt of any more jokes. He didn't even want to be Jamie Johnson any more.

Maybe he should give up playing football and do sprinting instead. The athletics coach at school had said that he was quick enough to be a professional sprinter; that if he trained hard, he could go to the Olympics. . . But Jamie didn't like athletics. He loved football. He always would. And Bryn and Tyler were trying to stop Jamie doing what he loved most.

The wind was tapping angrily at Jamie's window now. Jamie could almost hear it whistling, taunting him, just like the others had done in the playground:

He's short, he's sad, he doesn't have a dad. . .
He's Jamie Johnson, Jamie Johnson. . .

As he pulled the duvet tight around himself, Jamie felt the sting of a tear prick the corner of his eye.

But, as he wiped it away, a surge of determination sprang up inside him.

He knew exactly why Bryn and Tyler targeted him: he played left wing in The Grove's school team and left wing was Tyler Forbes's position too. So, as long as Jamie was playing, Tyler couldn't get in the team. He and Bryn, being best mates, had made a plan to try and get him out . . . to try and stop him playing football altogether.

Jamie's granddad, Mike, had warned him this would happen; that he would always be a target for people who weren't as good as him.

They were jealous of his talent. They were jealous because they wished they could do the things with a football that Jamie could do.

"Never give up," Mike had always told him. "Just keep coming back for more. And if someone ever tries to make you feel small, you stand up for yourself!"

Jamie turned over and clenched his fists into his chest.

Bryn and Tyler wanted to stop Jamie doing what he did best. They wanted to stop him playing. But Jamie wouldn't let them. No one would ever stop him playing football.

It was time for Jamie to stand up for himself.

③

The Sandwich

Friday 15 October

When the bell went and everyone went outside for break, Jamie decided to stay in the classroom for a bit. Hugo was staying inside too. Maybe Jamie would see what Hugo was doing at the weekend.

It wasn't as if Jamie didn't have other mates outside school – of course he did. For a start, he had Jack – the best mate in the world. She was way cooler than any of the kids at The Grove.

But at The Grove, Jamie pretty much just had Hugo.

He and Hugo had kind of just been thrown together. They lived quite near each other and, by the end of the first week at The Grove, they were the only two who didn't belong to any of the gangs. So they decided to form their own gang. Of two.

They didn't exactly make a scary pair, but at least it meant they both had someone to go around with, and they always sat next to each other at lunch.

Not that they had a whole lot in common.

Jamie was quite shy, especially with people he didn't know that well, and Hugo . . . well, there was no other way to say it . . . Hugo was a little weird.

He took delight in the strangest things. Bogies were a particular delicacy for him, whether they were his or someone else's!

But, above all else, Hugo's number-one speciality was farting. He could do all sorts: silent, potent, eggy . . . but he was a real expert at the loud ones. His best ones sounded like a duck quacking!

He was so proud of each fart he did that he wanted to tell the whole world about them.

"Can you smell it yet?" he'd ask Jamie when he'd let rip, his eyes gleaming with excitement.

If Jamie had a pound for every time that Hugo had asked him to "pull his finger", Jamie would already be a millionaire!

Jamie stared as Hugo carefully unwrapped his sandwiches. Jamie felt like a scientist studying a wild monkey.

As soon as the sandwiches came out of the silver foil, the smell immediately invaded Jamie's nostrils.

They smelled like poo! They reeked so badly Jamie thought that he was going to heave. Then he saw that brown, jellied juices were beginning to drip down the side of the bread. . .

"Man! What's in that sandwich?" Jamie yelled, covering his nose as Hugo tucked in. "It looks like dog food!"

Hugo Bogson just stared back at Jamie. He didn't say anything. Instead he just smiled, and then he took another big bite of his sandwich.

"I'm sorry, Hugo, but that's rank!" laughed Jamie. "I'm going to play football!"

And with that, Jamie practically sprinted out of the room.

It was a cold, wet day and the air from Jamie's mouth immediately froze into white clouds in front of him. They were so thick it looked as if Jamie was breathing out smoke.

Jamie thrust his hands into his pockets to keep them warm. Most of the other kids were wearing gloves. But Jamie didn't like wearing them. They made his hands feel trapped.

The match had already started and the players on either side were running about after the ball like madmen. None of them were holding their positions. They just all swarmed around after the ball.

In the middle of the playground, someone had

been sick and the caretaker had put a load of sawdust over the top of it to soak up the liquid.

"What's the score?" Jamie asked, standing on the side of the playground. "Which side shall I go on?"

He wished that someone would just ask him to be on their side. He wished that for once he could be part of a gang at The Grove. Not always an outsider. If his mum had listened to him and sent him to Kingfield with Jack, then he wouldn't have any of these stupid problems.

"Who said you can play anyway?" shouted Bryn, coming across to confront Jamie.

"Free country!" Jamie shouted back. "Who made you king?"

"Right," shouted Bryn, "let's get him!"

Suddenly Bryn and Tyler sprinted over to the heap of wet sawdust. Then they grabbed some of it in their gloves!

And now they were running towards Jamie with balls of sawdust and sick pressed in the palms of their gloves, ready to release. It was as if they'd invented a new game called sickball! Except Jamie didn't have any weapons of his own.

But he had something else. His pace.

Jamie immediately hit top speed, twisting and swerving in different directions to avoid his pursuers.

Bryn and Tyler knew there was no way they would be able to catch Jamie in a straight race, but they had two against one, so they split into different directions to make sure that they could trap him.

Soon they were coming at Jamie from either side. He was cornered. He had to stop.

"OK, guys," he said, putting his hands up. "You got me. But you don't have to do this, you know."

"Course we don't have to do it, you idiot!" Tyler sniggered, looking at the disgusting parcel of sick and sawdust in his glove. "We *want* to do it!"

"Guys, really. . . Trust me, you don't," said Jamie, looking to his left and his right as an idea suddenly came into his head. It was such a good idea that he couldn't help but start smiling.

"What are you laughing at?" shouted Bryn angrily. "This'll shut you up!"

And simultaneously, he and Tyler Forbes launched their sick missiles at him.

Jamie had half a millisecond in which to work, if he was to get his plan right. As soon as he saw the rockets heading towards him, he ducked as quickly as he could. He could feel the breeze of the sickballs whoosh over the top of his head.

The rockets just missed him, and each other, as they crossed paths in the air. Instead, they carried on their journeys. By the time Bryn and Tyler actually realized what was happening, it was too late! Their own sickballs were heading straight for each other and there was no time for them to get out of the way!

SPLAT!!

The sickballs smashed into their faces and oozed down the side of their cheeks. Some went in Bryn's hair and it looked as if some had even gone into Tyler's mouth!

While they were still in shock, spitting sawdust out of their mouths and wiping sick off their faces, Jamie stood up and pointed at them.

"Who's stupid now?" he laughed. "Serves you right!"

Then he started running back to the school building. It was almost time for lessons.

He knew they'd chase after him.

But he also knew they'd never catch him. Not today, anyway. . .

4

Glory Days

Saturday 16 October

"And none of your secret fish and chip dinners on the way home, Dad!" Jamie's mum shouted to her dad, Mike, as he and Jamie headed off to the Hawkstone game. "I know what you two get up to!"

"OK, love," replied Mike, full of sincerity.

But as they left the house, he gave Jamie a wink and a smile.

"What she doesn't know won't hurt her!" they said in unison, as soon as they were out of earshot.

Jamie absolutely loved going to Hawkstone games with Mike. They didn't have enough money to get a season ticket, but in a way, that meant that the games they did get to go to were even more special.

Football had linked Mike and Jamie pretty much since the day Jamie was born.

Mike had bought Jamie his first football when he was two years old. It was the best present that Jamie had ever had.

For Jamie, what set Mike apart from everyone else, what made him so cool, was that he had once been a professional footballer for Hawkstone. Jamie thought that, since Mike had done it, maybe there was a chance he could do it too.

As they walked the three-kilometre journey to the ground and joined the hordes of other fans making the same pilgrimage, Jamie felt really mature. Almost like an adult.

When Jamie was younger, Mike used to carry him all the way to the ground on his shoulders. He was a really strong man and Jamie loved that feeling of being so high in the air, looking down on everyone else. And the funny thing was that, even now, when he was with Mike, Jamie still felt six feet tall.

"Here it is," said Mike. "Here's that photo I was telling you about."

Mike had stopped by one of the large photos next to the catering area inside the ground.

Jamie looked at the photo and the plaque underneath it, which read:

Victorious Hawks – United's First-Ever Youth Cup Winning Team

"This was the day we won the Youth Cup," Mike said, shaking his head wistfully. "I can't believe that was forty years ago. . . I look about as old as you look now!"

"Which one's you, Mike?" said Jamie, searching the faces of the players for one who looked like a younger version of his granddad.

"That's me," said Mike, pointing to a big tank of a player in the back row. "Those were my glory days, JJ."

Jamie looked at the photo. His eyes zoomed in to the picture of his grandfather as a young footballer. He looked so young, so strong . . . so happy.

Jamie wanted to be just like Mike and maybe, one day, as good as him.

"Shall I tell you what the trick of life is, Jamie?" said Mike, putting his hand on his grandson's shoulder. "Realizing that sometimes you only get one shot at something. So when that chance comes along, you'd sure as hell better take it."

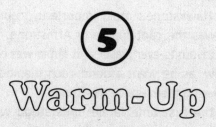

⑤
Warm-Up

Jamie and Mike always liked to get to their seats in time for the warm-up because it meant they got to see a different side to the players than the one they saw during the game.

They caught a glimpse of the players' *real* characters – those who liked a laugh and those who were deadly serious. They could see who was mates with who by the way they paired off to do their stretches . . . and they could also see who had the most skills, as the warm-up was a chance to show off!

There was no doubt that Hawkstone's most skilful player was their young midfielder, Glenn Richardson.

His passing vision was unbelievable. Jamie reckoned he could have even played the game blindfolded and still known exactly where all his teammates were on the pitch.

But Hawkstone's most important, inspirational player was the captain, Harry Armstrong. He was Jamie's favourite-ever player and Jamie was watching him now, as he went around each member of his team, geeing them up for the game.

For the first time Jamie understood what the pundits meant when they said a player would "run through brick walls".

Harry Armstrong was so brave he would make the brick wall feel scared!

The only Hawkstone player who didn't seem to be particularly interested in the warm-up was the goalkeeper, Leon Tibbs.

Tibbs was a bit of a Hawkstone legend, but in the last few seasons there was no doubt he'd put on some weight. And he was rude to the fans too. Jamie and Jack had once seen him in the street and asked for his autograph. Tibbs had just laughed at them and said, "You two couldn't afford *my* signature!"

Jamie could see that Tibbs wasn't even allowing the mascot to take proper shots at him. The mascot looked so scared that he wasn't even confident enough to give the ball a proper kick. What was the point in that?!

"See if you can pick up some tips today for that game of yours against Kingfield in a couple of weeks," Mike said to Jamie as Hawkstone kicked off in front of them. "The bigger the game, the better you should play."

Jamie nodded and tried to force a smile.

He felt bad because, on the way to the ground, he'd told Mike about his big upcoming school match against Kingfield – The Grove's fiercest rivals. Jamie had explained that it was the biggest match of the whole season and that sometimes the local newspaper even did a report on the game. . . And then Jamie had asked Mike not to come!

"Sometimes knowing that you're watching makes me a bit nervous," Jamie had said, trying to put into words why Mike had to stay away. "I just end up trying to impress you and then I don't play my normal game."

He'd been worried about Mike's reaction because he knew how much Mike loved to watch him play. But Mike had just said, "No worries. Whatever makes you happy, JJ."

That was why Jamie respected Mike so much: he always understood.

Jamie and Mike got back home from the game to find a note from his mum on the kitchen table.

Hiya Dad and Jamie!
   Did you have a good game? I heard you won! Does that mean you'll be in a good mood tomorrow, then?
   I'm popping out to meet Jeremy from work. And no, before either of you ask, it's not a date! We're just friends!!
   Anyway, there's food in the fridge. Have fun, you two mischief-makers!!

Love, Mum/Karen xx

Jamie and Mike immediately did a high five. They were both stuffed from the fish and chips on the way home, but the fact that Jamie's mum was out meant that they didn't have to pretend they were still hungry!

They sat on the sofa, and while Mike watched the golf, Jamie started reading the match programme from that day's game. He'd bought it with his own money. He always did whenever he went to a game, and he kept all the ones he'd ever bought. After every game, as soon as he got home, he read it from cover to cover, memorizing every word. Every fact.

It was strange, really. At school, Jamie hated reading. All his teachers spent their whole time trying to get him to read. But they wanted him to read about boring stuff like wars and poetry. If they'd just given him a Hawkstone programme, he could have read it quicker than anyone else. And sometimes he even learned good words from them too. Like "prodigy". That meant someone who had amazing skills.

Jamie wanted to be a football prodigy . . . playing for Hawkstone United . . . destined for the big time. . .

In the centre pages of the programme, there was a wicked poster of Harry Armstrong. Jamie carefully opened the staples and pulled it out, making sure not to rip it. He was going to stick it on his wall, alongside all the other Harry Armstrong posters he already had.

At the front of the programme, there was also a message from the Hawkstone chairman, Tony Walsh.

Jamie always read Tony Walsh's message to the fans because it was the only way he found out what the chairman's plans were for the club. Tony Walsh never did interviews on the TV, so Jamie didn't even know what he looked like! From what Jamie could tell from the programme, though, he seemed like a good bloke.

...I'm delighted to say that our big Cup game against Tolford in a couple of weeks has already completely sold out.

With your fantastic support behind us plus our plans to sign some of the best players from around the world, I believe that we are on schedule to achieve our aim of Champions League football for Hawkstone within the next five years.

Together we can do it.

And, as I always say, I may be the chairman, but this will always be <u>your</u> Club.

Tony Walsh
Chairman
Hawkstone United Football Club

Jamie closed his eyes and imagined his dream world. One day, he would be playing for Hawkstone United in the Champions League. . . He could see himself doing it . . . he wanted it so badly. . .

Make it happen, he said to himself and anyone else who could hear his thoughts. *Please . . . make it happen.*

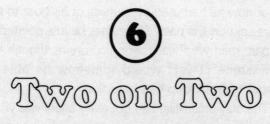

6

Two on Two

Sunday 17 October

As he sprinted down to meet his best mate, Jack, for their weekly kickaround, Jamie ran over yesterday's Hawkstone game in his mind.

Glenn Richardson had scored the only goal of the game with a wicked half-volley from the edge of the area. Hawkstone were having a seriously good season. They were even pushing for a European place.

But for Jamie, almost as interesting as watching the game had been watching Mike *watching* the game.

Jamie had tracked his reactions to everything that had happened to see if he could pick up any tips. After all, it wasn't as though many people had a granddad who had been a professional.

Generally, Mike didn't say much while the game was going on; he just chewed his gum and clapped the occasional pass, explaining to Jamie how the player had leant back so the ball went higher in the air or how he had used the outside of his boot to put more spin on the pass. Sometimes he just pointed to a spare man who was making a run, as though the Hawkstone players would somehow be able to telepathically pick up his suggestion.

The only time Mike had got really angry was when one of the opposition players pretended he had been fouled to try and get one of Hawkstone's players sent off. As the player was writhing around on the ground, faking an injury, Mike had got up out of his seat and shouted, "Get on with the game, you cheat!"

A few minutes later, after he'd chilled out a bit, he'd turned to Jamie and said, "I hope you never do that, JJ. A bit of class goes a long way in this game – remember that."

"Here he is," said Jack, as Jamie arrived in Sunningdale Park. "The man they're all talking about!"

"What d'you mean?" asked Jamie, blasting the ball at Jack, who was already in goal with her gloves on. "Who's talking about me?"

"The boys in the team at Kingfield," she said. "They've all heard of you. They were discussing how they're going to stop you in the match. . . Apparently they've made a special plan to put you off your game!"

"Tell them not to bother," smiled Jamie, bending in a shot. "No one's managed to stop me yet!"

"It's seriously wicked at Kingfield, you know," Jack called as she dived away to her right. She was a good 'keeper: brave and agile. "You should definitely ask your mum again about moving schools – you'd love it there. How's this week been at The Grove? Any better?"

Jamie was desperate to join Kingfield but, right now, his pride wouldn't let him admit it to Jack.

"Yeah, much better," Jamie lied. "You know those two bullies that I was telling you about? Well, I taught them a lesson on Friday. I'd just had enough, so I sorted them both out. They were crying like babies at the end . . . you should've seen it!'

"Really?" said Jack, a little surprised. "You took on both of 'em?"

"Course I did!" insisted Jamie. "Took 'em both down!"

"Wow," said Jack, taking off her gloves. "You must be really strong. Let me feel your muscles, then!"

"Nah – get off!" said Jamie as Jack started tickling him in his armpit. "Jack! Get off me!" he squealed with a mixture of pleasure and pain as she continued. His laugh was so high-pitched, he almost sounded like a girl!

But then something made Jamie shut his mouth. His voice caught in his throat.

27

On the far side of the park, walking straight towards him and Jack, were Bryn Staunton and Tyler Forbes.

They were kicking a ball to each other, looking pretty hard as they strode forward. When they teamed up together they made a pretty menacing pair.

In the beginning, when he'd first joined The Grove, Jamie had sucked up to them to try and get in their gang but, because he played in the same position as Tyler, they weren't having any of it. They had decided that he was enemy number one.

And now after he'd got the better of them with the sickballs on Friday, they were out for revenge.

"Let's go," said Jamie, panicking as he turned to face Jack.

"Go? We've only just got here! What you chatting about?" she laughed. "Scared you won't be able to score against me, are you? Worried you're gonna flop?!"

"I'm serious, Jack! We need to go! Remember those two that I said I took down? Well, now they're coming here and they're gonna—"

But it was too late.

Bryn and Tyler had arrived.

"Playing with a girl, eh?" mocked Bryn. "Yeah, that's about all you're good enough for!"

"You're gonna get some beats on Monday, man . . . you best believe!" threatened Tyler, smacking his fist into his hand as Jamie started to back away.

"OK," Jack said suddenly, surprising all three of the boys. "How's about we sort this out with a quick game of two on two?"

"Against you two? A midget and a girl! We'll destroy you," laughed Bryn.

"Maybe you will," smiled Jack, calmly. "But, if *we* win, you leave Jamie alone. Deal?"

"If you win, I'll run down the street naked!" shouted Bryn. Then he and Tyler started laughing, giving each other high fives.

"Er, I don't think anyone wants to see that," countered Jack. "Look, deal or no deal?"

"I'll tell you what the deal is," Bryn snapped, coming up right next to Jack and Jamie, aggressively staring them both in the eye. "You win – fine, we leave him alone, won't touch him no more. . . But if *we* win, he never plays football at school again. Ever. And Tyler takes his place in the school team."

"Nice one, bruv!" said Tyler, touching fists with Bryn.

"So that's the deal," Bryn said, turning back to Jack. "You still want it?"

"That doesn't even make sense," Jamie interrupted. He was getting annoyed at everyone talking about him as though he wasn't there. "What do I tell the coach when he asks why I'm not playing? And what sport am I supposed to do, if I don't play football?"

"Who cares?" said Bryn. "That's your problem."

"How about basketball?!" teased Tyler. They both collapsed into laughter again at the thought of little Jamie Johnson trying to do a slam dunk!

"Well, then?" asked Bryn impatiently. "What's it gonna be?"

Jamie and Jack looked at each other. Jamie shook his head. It was too big a risk. He *had* to be able to play football at school. It was what he lived for and his best chance of getting a professional club to spot his talent.

"Deal!" said Jack, completely ignoring Jamie. "Let's do it."

"What are you doing?" Jamie whispered angrily to Jack as they retreated into their own territory to organize their goal with their jumpers. "If I can't play football at school, I may as well—"

"Chill out, will ya, JJ?" said Jack, confidently bouncing the ball down on the ground. "What are you worried about? You sorted 'em out at school. Now you can sort 'em out again!"

"Jack, I was lying, it wasn't exactly like I—"

"Come on, JJ!" said Jack. "How many times have we ever lost a two v two?"

They looked at each other and then Jamie grinned.

"Never," he smiled. "Let's do it."

⑦

Sunday Best

Right from the very first kick of the match, when Jamie flicked the ball into the air, did an around-the-world, then back-heeled it to Jack, Bryn and Tyler simply could not get the ball off Jamie.

Even when the two of them paired up to both man-to-man mark him, it made no difference!

He was too quick, too skilful, too agile . . . too good.

The score had reached 12 – 1 before an exhausted Bryn Staunton finally said the magic words.

"All right, fair play, you win," he conceded, shaking Jack and Jamie's hands. "We'll leave the guy alone. And Tyler, I ain't being funny, mate, but I reckon you should find a new position. You ain't ever going to be as good as Jamie. He's got some serious skills!"

That Sunday afternoon, perhaps for the first time, Bryn Staunton and Tyler Forbes began to fully understand the talent that Jamie Johnson had for football.

This was not a normal boy. This was not just *some kid* who liked to play football.

This was a very special talent, and to take it on – to try to beat it – was stupid, not to say impossible.

Jamie didn't say a word to them after the game. There was no need. His feet had done all the talking.

Together, Jamie and Jack hadn't just beaten Bryn and Tyler; they had destroyed them.

After Bryn and Tyler had gone, Jamie and Jack sat down on their favourite bench to bask in their victory. They had had some good wins in Sunningdale but none as satisfying as this. Bryn had even asked Jamie to play on his side in break next week.

And Jamie knew that none of this would have happened had it not been for Jack. He had been ready to run away. It was only because she'd stood up to them that Jamie had had the confidence to do the same.

"Here," said Jamie. "Give me your key ring for a sec."

"What for?"

"Just give it here, will you?"

When Jack handed it over, Jamie pointed the sharp edge at the wood and, very carefully, started etching some letters into the bench.

J & J 4EVER, he carved.

*

As he went to bed that night, in his mind Jamie replayed some of the moves that he'd used in the match against Bryn and Tyler. In particular, he was pleased with the nutmeg he'd done on Tyler on his way to slotting home one of the eleven goals he'd scored in the game.

The nutmeg had been so perfect that even Bryn had shouted "*Nuts!*" And he was on Tyler's team!

Jamie reached over to set his alarm for school. It was ten-thirty on a Sunday night. Normally at this time, his stomach would be tight, and he would be nervously anticipating going back to school the next morning, dreading that buzzer going off and the journey to The Grove in the freezing morning fog.

But tonight Jamie had none of those worries. In fact, after the lesson he'd taught Bryn and Tyler on the football pitch this weekend and then Bryn's invitation for him to play on their side in break, Jamie was actually looking forward to school tomorrow. Well, almost, anyway. . .

Turning the Tables

Monday 18 October

"Oi, Jamie! Over here!

Jamie had his tray and was looking for somewhere to sit at lunch. He heard someone calling his name but he didn't know where in the dining hall the voice was coming from. Then Bryn got up off his bench and started flailing his arms around to catch his attention.

"Jamie!" he shouted. "Over here!"

This is beautiful, Jamie thought to himself as he carried his tray over, *seriously beautiful*.

"Oi, shift up, will you?" Bryn said to Tyler. "He needs some room to sit down."

As soon as Jamie sat down, the talk turned to the

match against Kingfield School, which was only just over a week away now.

"We gotta do 'em!" announced Bryn. "They reckon they're so hard. We gotta teach them a lesson!"

Jamie looked to the end of the table and saw Shaun McGiven eating his lunch in silence. McGiven was probably the quietest boy in the whole year. His skin was so pale that sometimes he reminded Jamie of a ghost. But if you put that boy on a football pitch, he was guaranteed to score you a goal. He was the best striker Jamie had ever played with.

"Oi, Bryn," said Jamie, suddenly feeling pumped with confidence. "Don't worry about Kingfield, mate. Just give me and McGiven the ball and we'll do the rest!"

All the boys started laughing and punching their fists on the table.

Jamie smiled. It felt good to be on the inside.

There was only one problem, and Jamie knew he'd have to sort it out sooner or later.

Hugo Bogson.

Thursday 21 October

After school on Thursday, Bryn, Jamie and the rest of the boys were all standing at the bus stop waiting to catch the bus into town to go to the arcade when

Hugo Bogson started walking towards them.

He even walked in a slightly weird way, bouncing a little too high off the ground, almost as though he were skipping.

"Do you want to come over to mine?" Hugo asked Jamie as the bus drew nearer.

Jamie could already hear the muffled laughter that Hugo's presence had brought about from the rest of the gang. They thought he was a complete idiot. He'd heard them refer to him as a "mentalist" and "freak boy".

Jamie knew that this was an important moment. He'd just got in with the others and, together, they had won every match at break-time this week. He was starting to get really popular. He couldn't blow it now.

"Come over to yours?" Jamie said. "No way! Your house stinks, man!"

Jamie turned and did high fives with everyone. They couldn't stop laughing as they watched Hugo Bogson walk away, head down, with his feet now barely lifting off the ground.

But even while he was still laughing, as he watched Hugo disappear out of sight, Jamie couldn't help but feel a little bit guilty at the same time.

⑨
The Overhead Kick

Sunday 24 October

"I'm telling you, we've got some seriously good players!" Jack was saying as the banter ahead of The Grove–Kingfield match notched up another gear. The game was only two days away now and it was all they had talked about this weekend.

"Our captain, right, Dillon Simmonds, is the hardest player I've ever seen," Jack boasted. "I reckon he eats glass for breakfast! And Ollie, our midfielder, is seriously brave. He's a good guy too. I reckon you'd like him."

Jamie didn't like the thought of Jack having other friends. Especially ones that he didn't know.

"Plus we've got a wicked striker," said Jack, saving one of Jamie's long-range lobs. "He's called Ash. You should tell your defenders to watch out for him! He's the quickest runner in the whole of our year. . . He's almost as quick as you!"

Jamie smiled. He liked it when Jack gave him compliments. But it was true. He'd never yet met anyone who was as fast as him. Sometimes he wondered if anyone was!

"Yeah, well, bet he doesn't score as many goals as Shaun McGiven!" Jamie hit back. "That boy is a killer in the area, I'm telling you."

"Bet he does!" Jack shot back. "Ash can do overhead kicks! He's even taught me how to do them!"

"Yeah, right!" laughed Jamie.

They'd been playing in the park together for years, and neither of them had ever managed to do a proper overhead kick. They'd always ended up falling on their backs and laughing through the pain at how rubbish their attempts had been!

"I can't even do an overhead kick and I'm a *winger*," said Jamie. "You're only a '*keeper*'!"

"Wanna bet?" Jack challenged. "Milkshakes?"

"Done," said Jamie. Only now was he starting to have any doubts – Jack always won their bets. Still, he could hardly imagine that Jack had learned how to do an overhead kick. This bet had to be his. He'd get an extra large milkshake to teach her a lesson!

They spat on their hands and shook them.

And then, without saying another word, Jack

tossed the ball into the air and, as it dropped, she launched her body towards it.

And sure enough, she produced the most amazing overhead kick! It was an absolutely perfect strike . . . the ball went miles!

"No way!" Jamie shouted. "Do it again!"

"Why?" laughed Jack, leaping back up to her feet. She didn't seem to be hurt at all. "You think it was a fluke?!"

"Just do it again. That was the best overhead kick I've ever seen. Go on! Do it!"

And so, just like before, Jack tossed the ball into the air and produced an awesome overhead kick! It didn't even look like she was trying!

"OK, you have to teach me!" Jamie begged, with a mixture of jealousy and excitement. "I'm serious! Teach me now! Please!"

"OK, but only if you promise not to use it against Kingfield – Ash'll kill me otherwise!"

"I promise . . . whatever! I just have to learn how to do that!"

"Fine," said Jack. "But when you're a big star and everything, you remember who taught you how to do an overhead kick!"

Jamie smiled while Jack picked up the ball and talked him through exactly how to do an overhead kick.

"See, at the moment you're too worried about hitting the ground when you come back down.

You're thinking about that instead of focusing on the ball," she explained.

"You've just got to relax," she said. "It's all in the timing. . . Trust me."

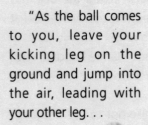

"As the ball comes to you, leave your kicking leg on the ground and jump into the air, leading with your other leg. . .

"Then keep your eyes completely fixed on the ball, right through until you strike it. . .

40

"Strike the ball with your laces . . . and still keep your eyes on it!

"Then, after you've got in your shot, just use your arms to break your fall. That way, you'll be up quickly to celebrate your goal!"

41

⑩

Standing Up

Monday 25 October

Jamie was just telling Bryn and Tyler about his overhead kicks when, out of the corner of his eye, he saw Hugo Bogson walking around the dining hall with his tray piled high with ravioli. The gloopy red sauce was trickling over the side of his plate.

Jamie could see Hugo's eyes scanning the room. Then, as he spotted Jamie, his eyes lit up and he hurried towards him, like a faithful dog that has just spotted its owner.

But Jamie looked away and carried on talking to Bryn.

"You can do overhead kicks?!" Bryn was saying. "Seriously? Show us how to do them, then!"

Jamie was only partially concentrating on the conversation because the rest of his brain was registering the fact that, at the last minute, Hugo had veered away from Jamie's table.

Finally, Jamie thought to himself. *Finally, he's got the message.*

It was harsh – and Jamie couldn't help feeling a bit sorry for Hugo, who was sitting all by himself on the other side of the dining hall – but things had changed now and the sooner Hugo understood that, the bet—

"Oi, Jamie!" Bryn was half-shouting now. "So are you gonna show us how to do overhead kicks or what?!"

*

Match v Kingfield tomorrow.
Kick-off 2.30.
Coach leaves at 1 p.m. from the front gate.
Clean kits, please!
Mr Bolitho

Jamie read the notice three times and wrote down all the details in his school diary. He had to be right on time for tomorrow. Preparation was everything.

Jamie looked at his watch and sprinted to class for English but, even though he was four minutes late, the teacher was not there yet.

It was 2.04 and, with no sign of Mr Leyburn, everyone was starting to mess around. It was almost like a party in the classroom.

Bryn was jeering loudly as Hugo Bogson went around the class trying to find a spare seat. Every time he tried to sit down next to someone, they simply said, "Sorry, this seat's taken."

Finally, Hugo found a seat at the front, right next to the teacher's desk.

He took off his rucksack and went to sit down, but just before his bum connected with the chair, Bryn whipped it away.

Hugo went crashing to the floor and, as he hit the deck, the whole class erupted in thunderous laughter.

Then, while Hugo was vulnerable, Bryn and Tyler piled in to pinch him on his cheek and his bum.

"Enjoy your trip?!" they mocked, pinching away painfully at him and flicking his ears.

"Get off," Hugo protested, trying in vain to push their hands away. "Leave me alone! What have I done to you?"

"What's the matter?" shouted Bryn. "We're only having a laugh! Can't the weirdo take a joke?!"

Now they were emptying Hugo's rucksack and tipping the contents all over the floor.

"OK, enough now," Jamie said, suddenly standing up. He knew this wasn't right.

Bryn and Tyler looked up at him. Then they started

laughing and continued where they had left off.

"Hold him down, Tyler," shouted Bryn excitedly. "I'm gonna fart on his head!"

"I mean it, guys. Leave him alone," Jamie repeated, firmly.

Bryn stood up and walked towards Jamie. Jamie took half a step back. He wondered if things were about to go back to the bad old days.

"And what do you care about freak boy for, anyway, Johnson?" he barked. "You don't have to pretend to be his mate any more now!"

"He's all right," said Jamie, standing up as tall as he could. He came up to Bryn's neck. "He's not done anything to you lot."

"Yes, he has!" shouted Tyler, who now had Hugo in a headlock. "He's offended me with his BO! He smells like a tramp!"

"Well, I think he's all right," countered Jamie. "So you better leave him alone!"

"Or what?" Tyler bellowed. This was getting serious now.

"Yeah," said Bryn. "Or what?"

Jamie's mind suddenly went horribly blank. *Or what*? He didn't know the answer to that question. What could he possibly threaten Bryn and Tyler with? He tried to imagine what Jack would do in this situation. She never lost her cool. . .

"Or I don't teach you overhead kicks and I'll never

play on your team in break ever again," Jamie suddenly blurted out with as much confidence as he could muster. He wondered if they could see his chest pounding through his shirt. He could feel his heart racing.

Tyler looked to Bryn and Bryn looked to Jamie. Jamie nodded to show he was serious.

For a couple of seconds there was absolute silence.

Then Bryn stormed up to Hugo and pulled his clenched fist back. Hugo flinched, preparing himself for the punch that would knock him out. But instead, he only felt Bryn's arm sweep around his neck in a kind of brotherly embrace.

"What are you worried for, Boggy, me old chum?" said Bryn, slapping Hugo very hard on his back. "Like Jamie says . . . you're all right by us. . ."

Match Day!

Tuesday 26 October

Kingfield v The Grove
Kick-Off 2.30

12.55 p.m.

Jamie was just getting on the coach to go to the match against Kingfield when he heard his name being called.

At first Jamie ignored it because he recognized the voice. But the calls kept coming.

"Jamie! Wait!" Hugo Bogson was shouting. He was so near now that it was impossible for Jamie not to acknowledge him. He just hoped Hugo didn't embarrass him in front of everyone before the game. He needed all his confidence for this match.

"Hugo," said Jamie, turning around. "I'm in a rush, mate, we're just about to go to the—"

"I wanted to give you something," said Hugo, rummaging around in the bottom of his rucksack.

"Sorry, mate, I haven't got time," said Jamie. He wondered what kind of rubbish rested at the bottom of Hugo's rucksack. "We're leaving right now."

"Here you go!" said Hugo triumphantly, handing Jamie a package in a plastic bag. "These are for you."

"What is it?" asked Jamie suspiciously as he took hold of the package. If it was some of Hugo's "special" sandwiches, he might be sick on the spot.

"Open it!" smiled Hugo.

Jamie nodded and, very slowly, with extreme caution, he peered inside the plastic bag. Then he pulled out the contents.

He couldn't believe it.

In his hands, he was holding a brand new pair of shin pads. They were the best ones on the market!

"Wow!" said Jamie. "Why are you giving me these, Hugo? Not that I don't like them . . . or need them . . . they're wick—"

"Way I see it," said Hugo, "You stopped me from getting a kicking yesterday . . . thought maybe I could do the same for you today."

"I'll wear these for the match today!" smiled Jamie. "Thanks, Hugo."

"Pleasure," replied Hugo. "Now pull my finger!"

As Jamie stepped off the coach, arriving at Kingfield's pitches, he felt the same sensations in his body that he felt before every big game: a tingling combination of confidence, fear and excitement. The anticipation bubbled in his blood and the longing for a win – the need to succeed – tantalized his mind.

But today, the quickening of his pulse, the sudden shot of adrenaline into his veins seemed to be sending Jamie the message that something extra, something different might be afoot.

He sensed that today was going to be an important day in his football career. A special day, even.

The question was, why? And . . . how?

(12)

Game On!

2.18 p.m.

"Hi," said a player on the Kingfield team, as Jamie jogged out on to the pitch. He was the biggest boy Jamie had ever seen. Was he really only in Year Seven?

"My name's Dillon Simmonds," the boy said, politely, shaking Jamie's hand. "Listen, I've just lost one of my contact lenses. I was wondering if you could help me find it?"

"Sure," said Jamie, surprised at how nice this Dillon boy seemed. Maybe Jamie could even become mates with a couple of the Kingfield players.

Jamie got down and started looking in the grass for the contact lens. He was really good at finding things, so he was sure he would be able to help Dillon find his lens. Then Jamie realized he had been a bit rude; he hadn't even introduced himself!

"Oh, my name's Jamie, by the—"

Thump! Dillon Simmonds kicked Jamie really hard up his bum, sending him tumbling over on to his back.

"What did you do that for?" Jamie yelled. His bum really hurt. "I was just trying to—"

"I don't even wear contact lenses, you idiot!" Dillon howled with laughter. "And that's only the first time I'm gonna kick you today!"

"What's your problem?" said Jamie, getting up. He looked around him to see if there was any backup. There was none.

"You're my problem!" shouted Dillon, leering over him. "Oh, are you standing up now? I couldn't even tell! Why you so small then, Ginge? Is your dad a dwarf?!"

"Don't talk about my dad!" Jamie snarled. "You don't know nothing about my dad!"

Jamie was so angry now he wanted to punch this ugly idiot as hard as he could, right in the face.

"OOOOOOH! Raw nerve!!" laughed Dillon, walking back to the changing rooms. "Sorry to upset you, dwarf boy! See you out on the pitch!"

Jamie watched him go.

You'll pay for that, Dillon Simmonds, he promised himself. *You'll pay.*

Action Time

Kingfield 1 - 1 The Grove
A Khan, 7   S McGiven, 16
58 MINS PLAYED

Jamie had to admit it. This was one of the toughest matches he'd ever played.

Normally The Grove were way better than the other schools they came up against. With Jamie Johnson and Shaun McGiven up front, they had too much firepower for most teams to handle.

But today was different. Today, The Grove had come up against a team that were just as good as they were. It was going to be a seriously close game and everyone knew it.

Kingfield had taken an early lead through their top striker, Ashish Khan. Jack had warned Jamie about him and she had been right. He could seriously shift. He'd outpaced the entire Grove back line before sending a cheeky chip home to open the scoring.

But then, like any good team, The Grove had hit back quickly. Jamie had dribbled past four players and set up Shaun McGiven, who equalized with a trademark curler into the top corner.

And since then, the game had been really tight.

Even Jamie was finding it hard to make an impression. The main reason for that was Dillon Simmonds.

He was tracking Jamie wherever he went and, if he wasn't putting in dangerous, crunching tackles, he was taunting and teasing Jamie with his verbals. It was as though he really hated Jamie even though this was the first time they had ever met each other.

"Oi, Ginge, where did ya get those boots? The charity shop? Can't you afford a proper pair?" Dillon Simmonds smirked as he made a run past Jamie towards The Grove's goal. Didn't he know that defenders were supposed to stay at the back?

Jamie hadn't reacted to any of Dillon's cusses yet. He knew his time would come. He just had to wait. Until the time was right. Then he would show Dillon what true talent was. Show him that skill was way more powerful than brute for—

Suddenly the ball had rebounded to Dillon, who was standing thirty-five yards from The Grove's goal. Dillon powered forward, controlling the ball firmly on his chest. The ball bounced up above his head and then, as it dropped, out of nowhere Dillon pelted a ferocious left-foot volley at the goal. It was a massive strike . . . and it was on target!

Jamie couldn't bear to watch. As soon as the ball had been struck he could tell it was going to go all the way. It was way too hard and far too high for the Grove 'keeper to get anywhere near it.

It shot like a rocket straight into the top corner.

Dillon Simmonds, the big, stupid, psycho defender, had just scored an unbelievable solo goal. And didn't he know it. . .

Kingfield 2 - 1 The Grove

A Khan, 7	S McGiven, 16
D Simmonds, 61	

"Come on!!" Dillon shouted, his cheeks burning red with glory. He'd raced over to the corner flag and kicked it way out of the ground to celebrate his amazing goal.

"What do you think about that, then?!" he roared at the Grove players. "Have some of that!"

The Grove were losing.

Jamie hated losing. At anything. It didn't matter what it was: a game of cards, snakes and ladders, a computer game. Whatever he did, he had to win. But most of all, what he couldn't bear, what he couldn't accept, was losing at football.

Once, when Jamie had lost a big Cup game at his primary school, he had been so angry and upset that he hadn't eaten a thing for the whole of the rest of the day. His mum had got really cross, telling him that he was going to make himself ill, but Jamie had just ignored her. She didn't understand that losing at football was the worst thing in the world.

It started a rage in Jamie. A rage which could only be calmed by him proving them wrong. Him proving that *he* was number one. *He* was the best.

Now, as the ball bounced towards him, Jamie knew it was time for him to do something.

He gathered in the ball and went on a run. . .

As soon as he had the ball under control, Jamie's mind instantly rid itself of all the clutter that normally littered it. Now, with the ball at his feet, Jamie's brain was clear and free. Free for football. Programmed to play. Set to score.

Jamie turned on his turbo gear and raced forward with the speed of a panther.

He'd already sped past three players and was heading right for the heart of the Kingfield defence when Dillon Simmonds slashed him down with a violent foul.

Jamie had been stopped. But not for long.

Because now he had exactly what he wanted.

A free-kick. . .

A Big Decision

Kingfield 2 - 1 The Grove

A Khan, 7   S McGiven, 16

D Simmonds, 61

67 MINS PLAYED

Jamie stood and addressed the ball straight on. Then he took three steps back, stood up to his full height and puffed out his chest. He took a series of deep breaths as he visualized exactly what he wanted to do with this free-kick.

It was a fair way out – twenty-two yards from goal – so Jamie knew he had to go for swerve and power rather than curl and accuracy.

Jamie stared hard at the ball. He was thinking about Luiz Rodriguez. Rodriguez was a Portuguese winger and the best free-kick taker in the world. Jamie had spent the whole of last week watching his free-kicks on YouTube.

Watching the free-kicks in slow-motion, Jamie had noticed that, when he struck the ball, Rodriguez never used a full follow-through. He punched his boot ferociously through the ball but then, as soon as possible after he had made contact, he brought his foot back down to the ground. This seemed to unleash a movement in the ball that no other technique could produce. Perhaps it was something to do with the pressure in the ball? Either way, it was almost impossible to stop.

Now it was Jamie's turn to have a go. . .

Jamie took a deep, determined breath, followed by three powerful strides towards the ball.

Then he hit it with the maximum force his body possessed. He struck the ball perfectly on its valve, bringing his foot quickly back down to the ground after it had made contact.

Now, Jamie just stood and watched. He'd done his bit. The rest was up to the ball. . .

All the players on the pitch – and even the referee – were hypnotized by the movement of the ball in the air. They watched it arc towards its target.

The goalkeeper stood, paralysed, on his line, his

feet anchored to the ground. Jamie actually felt a bit sorry for him. How could you try to save a ball when you had no idea which direction it was going to move next?

Thwack! The ball hit the goalkeeper's right-hand post, halfway up! Now it was spinning furiously across the goal-line. Was it going to go in. . .? Or was it – *thud!* It hit the other post! And it bounced out!

It was unbelievable! None of the players had ever seen a shot hit *both* posts and then bounce out without going in! Every player stood open-mouthed, trying to work out the science of how it had actually been possible.

Every player, that is, apart from Shaun McGiven. He was already on the move. He chased smoothly and swiftly after the ball, catching it in an instant. He hungrily gobbled up the chance, clipping the ball home with a quick, powerful strike before anyone else had moved.

That's what made McGiven different from other players. He was a true finisher. A natural-born predator. And he'd just scored again!

Kingfield 2 - 2 The Grove

A Khan, 7	S McGiven, 16, 68
D Simmonds, 61	

Even though it was McGiven's name on the

scoresheet, Jamie still raised his arms proudly above his head in triumph. He nodded confidently in appreciation of his own skill. He even looked up to the sky in some form of acknowledgement. He knew that no one else on the pitch was capable of doing what he had just done with the football.

Suddenly Jamie felt his whole body being hoisted into the air.

"What a free-kick, Jamie!" Bryn Staunton was shouting. His bear hug from behind had lifted Jamie four feet off the ground! "That was just like Rodriguez! Awesome!"

"Course it was!" said Jamie, as Bryn finally put him down. "I taught him everything he knows!"

There were ten minutes of the match left and both teams were piling forward in search of the winner. There was glory on offer for whoever could snatch the final goal.

Jamie was desperate to get on the scoresheet himself and win the game for The Grove. He had a feeling that he still had a big role to play in this match. But as time ticked on, it was Kingfield who looked more and more likely to score a goal.

They had a corner.

"You all go up," Dillon Simmonds ordered his Kingfield teammates. "Don't worry about the ugly ginge; I'll handle him!"

Jamie hated being called Ginge. If he could just get on to the ball, he knew he could tear Dillon to shreds. But right now, the action was all happening at the other end.

As the corner was whipped into the centre of the area, Bryn Staunton and one of the Kingfield players rose to contest it in the air. It was a fifty-fifty tussle and, although the Kingfield player made the first connection with the ball, they clashed heads badly. It sounded like two coconuts being crashed together.

Jamie saw the Kingfield player slump to the ground. He looked in a really bad way . . . but the ball had been cleared straight to Jamie!

With everyone committed to the corner, there were only two outfield players in the Kingfield half. One big, strong defender called Dillon Simmonds and one small, swift, skilful winger called Jamie Johnson. . .

Now was the time. The time for Jamie to let his talent come tumbling out.

Jamie latched on to the ball and immediately turned to face Dillon Simmonds.

Then he channelled all his anger at Dillon into his legs and burst forward with the ball. He was travelling at his very top speed, jinking left and right, with amazing close skill.

Now the tables had turned; Jamie was the one who was teasing Dillon. But he was doing it with the ball. His pace and control was mesmerizing the big defender, who suddenly seemed to be struggling to even stay on his feet!

This way and that Jamie turned, each time slipping away from Dillon's lunges. Jamie was like a wet bar of soap that Dillon could never quite catch.

He wasn't just one step ahead of Dillon Simmonds; he was light years in front.

Finally, Jamie flew past Dillon. Dillon tried to kick him – of course he did – but the impact of his boot had no effect on Jamie. The shin pads protected him perfectly.

Now Jamie bore down towards goal. He only had to decide how he was going to finish this game; whether he would go around the 'keeper with the ball or just slot it past him from the edge of the area.

"Bang it! Shoot!" Jamie's teammates from The Grove were shouting. They knew Jamie never missed a one on one.

But while his teammates were yelling at the top of their voices, Jamie had noticed that the crowd on the sidelines had gone deadly quiet.

In fact, they weren't even watching the game. They were pointing back towards The Grove's penalty area. There was worry on their faces.

Jamie turned around to see that the Kingfield player who had gone up for the header from the corner was still lying on the ground. He hadn't moved.

Jamie knew something was not right. If players were rolling around in agony, it meant they were in pain, but if they were not moving, it meant that they might not even be conscious. . .

Almost without thinking, Jamie kicked the ball straight out of play. Yes, he was giving up a near-certain goal, but he knew that boy needed help.

As soon as the ball went out, a man sprinted on to the pitch towards the stricken boy. He immediately laid him on his side and put his finger on the boy's throat.

"Does anyone here know first aid?" he shouted. There was panic in his voice.

A Touch of Class

Kingfield 2 - 2 The Grove
A Khan, 7   S McGiven, 16, 68
D Simmonds, 61
FULL-TIME

The game had finished in a draw. A bit of Jamie couldn't help but wonder if he'd done the right thing.

He had had the glory there in his grip. One kick and he could have won the game. He might even have got his name in the paper. But at the same time, he knew that something really bad could have happened to that boy.

He'd call Mike on the way home to ask him whether he'd done the right thing. He hoped Mike would back him up. After all, he was the one who always told Jamie how important sportsmanship was. . .

A little cloud of sadness hovered over Jamie for a second. He wished Mike had been here to watch the game.

But there was no need for Jamie to worry. . .

Mike had been at the match all right – he'd had to wear a baseball cap and stand way over on the other side of the pitch, but there was no way he was going to miss watching Jamie play in a game like this.

And as he left the Kingfield grounds before anyone could recognize him, Mike had a very big smile on his face.

This match had proved something to him that, deep down, he had probably always known. . .

His grandson had both the talent and the character to be a very special footballer indeed.

Out in the car park, Jamie was just putting his new shin pads into his kitbag when he sensed someone's large presence loom next to him.

Jamie tensed his stomach muscles. What if it was Dillon coming to do him in?

"I think my son and I owe you a thank you . . . Jamie, is it?"

It was the man who had run on to the pitch to help the boy who'd got injured. He had on the nicest coat Jamie had ever seen.

"No probs," said Jamie. "Is he OK? Looked like a bad one."

"Ollie's fine." The man smiled. "But it could have been serious. The blow to his head knocked him clean out and his tongue was blocking his airway. . . It's just lucky you kicked the ball out when you did. Is there any way I can thank you?"

"It's fine," said Jamie. "Don't worry about it. I'm just glad he's OK."

"No, really. I mean it – it was a real touch of class, what you did. . . Trust me, I'll think of something," he said, getting into his car. It was a brand new Ferrari and it had the personalized number plate *THW1*!

Jamie stared at the car in awe. He wondered if he would ever get to just *sit* in a car like that, let alone own one!

"Hang on a minute," said the man, getting back out of his car. "Who do you support, Jamie?"

"Hawkstone United," said Jamie, proudly. "All the way."

"Good," smiled the man. "I was hoping you might say that . . . and where are you planning to watch the Cup game tomorrow?"

"I'm going to go to my granddad's. We always watch. . ."

"You could do that," said the man. "Or you and your family could come to the game as my guests. How would you like to be Hawkstone's mascot, Jamie? I'm the chairman, by the way. My name's Tony Walsh."

(16)

Leading out the Team

Wednesday 27 October

Just before he left the house to head to the Hawkstone ground, Jamie looked at himself in the mirror.

This was the face that thirty-seven thousand people would see on the pitch tonight.

Was he ugly, like that boy Dillon had said? Jamie didn't know the answer.

His mum had always told him that he was handsome and that the girls would be queuing up for him, whenever he wanted them. But then again, she was his mum, she would hardly tell him he was ugly, would—

"Do we have a Hawkstone mascot in the house?!"

Jamie smiled as he registered Mike's voice booming up the stairs.

"Come on, JJ, let's get this show on the road!" He laughed as Jamie appeared at the top of the stairs. "I don't think they'll delay the kick-off, even for a VIP guest like you!"

As he waited in the tunnel for the Hawkstone players to come out of their dressing room, a flutter of nerves shivered through Jamie. He couldn't believe he was here, in this ground, at the club of his dreams. He had prayed for this moment to happen all his life.

"Hello, mate," said Harry Armstrong, the Hawkstone captain, who was the first out of the dressing room. He shook Jamie's hand and said, "What's your name? I'm Harry."

Jamie almost laughed. He knew who Harry Armstrong was – he was his biggest fan! But what he was struggling to come to terms with was the fact that he was now actually meeting Harry Armstrong . . . *in real life*!

"I'm Jamie. Jamie Johnson."

"Nice to meet you, Jamie. So what do you want to be when you're older, then?"

"I'm going to be a footballer," said Jamie, feeling his confidence rise. "I'm going to play for Hawkstone alongside you!"

Harry Armstrong laughed and ruffled Jamie's hair. "Good for you, kid," he smiled. "I'll look forward to it!"

Then the referee – who had a very bald head and

very hairy legs – walked to the front of the line and shook hands with both captains. They all called each other by their first names, but none of them seemed like friends.

"Ready, lads, here we go!" bellowed Harry Armstrong.

Suddenly Harry grabbed Jamie's hand and began the walk out of the tunnel towards the pitch.

With every stride, the roar of the crowd got nearer and louder.

Now, as they strode out on to the pitch, the wall of noise belted Jamie's ears. It was the loudest sound he had ever heard.

At that moment, Jamie couldn't imagine that anything else was happening in the world. It seemed that everyone on earth was here, shouting their heads off, ready for the big game!

As Jamie led the team out with Harry Armstrong, he knew for sure that he had never been happier in his life.

There were cameras, commentators and thirty-seven thousand people all focusing their attention directly on Jamie. But Jamie no longer felt nervous. In fact, he felt the reverse. Maths tests made him nervous. Not football.

As he kicked his first ball on the Hawkstone pitch, a set of words kept repeating themselves in Jamie's mind.

The words seemed to be coming from every cell in his body: "This is where I belong. . . This is where I belong. . ."

Playing to the Crowd

"Jamie! Coin toss!" shouted Harry Armstrong.

He had remembered Jamie's name! Harry Armstrong actually remembered Jamie's name!

As they walked to the centre circle to toss the coin with the opposition, Jamie realized that Harry Armstrong was a lot bigger in person than he seemed on the TV. Jamie knew everything about him – that he was five-foot eleven, and weighed twelve stone. He even knew when his birthday was! (October thirtieth.) But it was only now, standing next to him, that Jamie properly felt the physical presence that Harry Armstrong exuded.

Jamie saw the look of steel in Harry's eyes, which

said that he would stop at nothing to achieve victory.

Jamie smiled. If Planet Earth was sending a football team to play against a team of aliens from outer space, he thought that Harry Armstrong should be Planet Earth's captain. That's how highly Jamie rated him.

While the photographer took a photo of Jamie and Harry Armstrong standing together by the centre spot, in the stands, Mike was filming every second.

"Don't worry about filming it, Dad," suggested Jamie's mum. "Just watch it – you'll enjoy it more."

Mike glanced at her and smiled. He was still using his old video camera even though the new phone that Jamie and his mum had bought him for his birthday had a wicked camera on it.

"It's not for *me*," Mike said. "It's for Jamie. You never know – one day, he might thank me."

"OK, let's get this over and done with, kid," Leon Tibbs growled as Jamie jogged towards his goal. Hawkstone's grumpy 'keeper was chomping his way through a mouthful of gum as he rolled the ball out to Jamie's feet.

Jamie nodded and did the lightest kick he could back into Tibbs's hands. He was too scared to do anything else.

"That's it," Tibbs shouted. "Just a couple more. Then you can go back to your daddy and I can get a proper warm-up."

Jamie felt his temples bristle with sweat. He didn't like it when people underestimated him. And he liked it even less when they talked about his dad.

With the next ball, Jamie tried a curler, hitting the ball a bit harder this time. Tibbs only just got across to make the save.

"Don't you dare try and score against me, titch," snarled Tibbs. "You're not good enough. End of story!"

Jamie began to feel his adrenaline kicking in as he heard a few people in the crowd start to notice him.

Tibbs gave Jamie a stern look as he rolled the ball back out to him.

Jamie teed himself up for a volley this time and belted it as hard as he could! Tibbs flung himself into the air and pushed it wide with the very tips of his fingers. It was a great piece of action.

Some of the crowd even clapped!

"One more time, kid. . ." Tibbs threatened. "Just try it one more time, and believe me, you won't know what's hit you!"

Jamie knew he shouldn't have done it, but he couldn't help it; the more the crowd clapped him, the more he wanted to please them.

Now Jamie did a chip. It was a beautiful little drifter of a shot which seemed to glide effortlessly through the air. Jamie could see the anger on Tibbs's face as he back-pedalled furiously to tip the ball on to the crossbar. Jamie had so nearly scored!

This was turning into a proper battle now and quite a few of the fans were getting to their feet to witness the contest.

Tibbs charged towards Jamie.

"See! I told you you'd never score against me! Now get off this pitch before I kick you off myself!" he yelled.

"OK! I'm going!" said Jamie. He could see the blood vessels in Tibbs's eyes starting to go red.

As Jamie started to walk off the pitch, some of the crowd even booed. They wanted him to stay on!

There was one more ball on the edge of the penalty area and Jamie was desperate to have another shot, but he knew that if he did, Tibbs would probably go so mental that he'd have a fit before the match had even started!

Jamie knew his time was up. He headed for the tunnel.

"Go home and ask your daddy to teach you some respect!" Leon Tibbs shouted after him.

Suddenly Jamie stopped walking. Now he was angry. Very angry.

Stuff you, Leon Tibbs, he thought to himself as he slowly turned around.

Then Jamie walked confidently up to the ball on the edge of the area and flicked it into the air, with his back still to goal. *You're the one who needs to learn some respect!*

Jamie controlled the ball on his chest, and let it fall back down to his thigh. Then he kneed it up into the air. . .

Focusing completely on the ball, Jamie launched his body up off the ground to meet it.

Jamie was lying completely flat in the air. His eyes were fixed firmly on the ball as he snapped first his right foot, then his left foot, back with ferocious pace over his head.

The contact was sweet and powerful. Hard and accurate. As Jamie dropped to the ground, the ball arrowed towards the goal. Jamie didn't even have to look around; he knew it was a beautiful overhead kick. His football senses told him so.

Jamie's shot fired like a cannonball straight into the corner of the net. And Leon Tibbs got nowhere near it. Even two Leon Tibbses wouldn't have kept it out!

The strike had so much power it came back out of the goal after it had gone in!

Jamie couldn't believe it! He had actually scored a goal at Hawkstone United!

The crowd immediately went berserk! The fans were celebrating as if Hawkstone had just won the Cup!

Jamie was in a daze of ecstasy, but before he had the chance to celebrate, he saw Leon Tibbs racing out of his goal, heading straight for him. . .

Jamie started to jog towards the tunnel, with Tibbs's shouts ringing in his ear.

"Oi, titch! Where d'you think you're going?" the 'keeper bellowed. "You stay right where you are!"

It was certainly lucky for Jamie that, seemingly from nowhere, Harry Armstrong suddenly appeared, putting his body between Tibbs and Jamie.

Even Tibbs knew not to mess with Harry Armstrong.

"Jamie looks like he's going be some player, doesn't he, Leon!" smiled Harry calmly. "Get your composure back, 'Keeps. We're kicking off in a second."

But Tibbs was still seething with anger at having been beaten by an eleven-year-old mascot.

"No one does that to me!" he snarled.

"Exactly," agreed Harry Armstrong. "Exactly. . ."

(18)

Remember the Name

As the two teams got ready to start the game, the stadium announcer's booming voice came on the tannoy.

"OK, before he goes, let's say a big thank you to our mascot for today, Jamie Johnson! And if what we've just seen is anything to go by, that is probably a name we should all remember!"

Jamie raised his hand, a little shyly.

He could not believe what had just happened! He had produced his best-ever piece of skill in front of thirty-seven thousand fans! It was almost as though being on this stage, playing on this pitch, had taken Jamie's talent to another level.

Then, slowly at first, from one pocket of supporters initially, but quickly spreading through the ground like a hungry fire, a chant got louder and louder until it seemed that every fan in the ground was on his feet singing the same words. . .

"One Jamie Johnson! There's only one Jamie Jooohhhnson. . . There's only ooone Jamieeee Johhhnson!"

Jamie's heart burned with pride. He loved the feeling of being cheered by so many people. He hoped they would never stop.

Confident now, he turned to wave to the crowd in every corner of the ground.

As the appreciation for him got louder and louder, Jamie smiled and leapt into the air, punching his fist skyward.

This was the first time that thousands of football fans stood up to applaud Jamie Johnson's talent. But they hadn't seen anything yet. This boy was born to play. . .

Acknowledgements

Thanks to:

The Erlicks and the Freedmans for all your support and encouragement.

Caspian Dennis, Ena McNamara and Oli Karger for your advice. And to Joanne too, when you had a few other things on your mind.

Ms Pluckrose and her team of secret agents at St Edward's. No throwing sickballs, please, you lot!

Hazel Ruscoe – this story is inspired by the ideas we had together.

Prezzo Restaurants and The Football Foundation for getting behind the Jamie Johnson series.

Sarah Stewart for your patience and insight.

And to the rest of the team at Scholastic for spotting Jamie's potential and giving him the chance to play…

Want to know what happens next? Follow the rest of Jamie Johnson's journey. . .

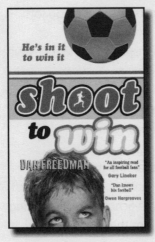

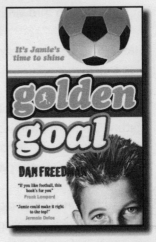

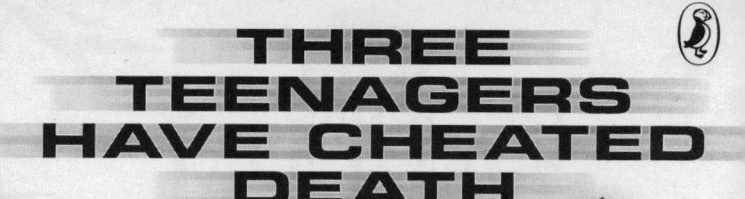

YOUNG SAMURAI
THE WAY OF FIRE

CHRIS BRADFORD

PUFFIN

For Charlie Viney, my agent

PUFFIN BOOKS

Published by the Penguin Group
Penguin Books Ltd, 80 Strand, London WC2R ORL, England
Penguin Group (USA) Inc., 375 Hudson Street, New York, New York 10014, USA
Penguin Group (Canada), 90 Eglinton Avenue East, Suite 700, Toronto, Ontario, Canada M4P 2Y3
(a division of Pearson Penguin Canada Inc.)
Penguin Ireland, 25 St Stephen's Green, Dublin 2, Ireland (a division of Penguin Books Ltd)
Penguin Group (Australia), 250 Camberwell Road, Camberwell, Victoria 3124, Australia
(a division of Pearson Australia Group Pty Ltd)
Penguin Books India Pvt Ltd, 11 Community Centre, Panchsheel Park, New Delhi – 110 017, India
Penguin Group (NZ), 67 Apollo Drive, Rosedale, North Shore 0632, New Zealand
(a division of Pearson New Zealand Ltd)
Penguin Books (South Africa) (Pty) Ltd, 24 Sturdee Avenue, Rosebank,
Johannesburg 2196, South Africa

Penguin Books Ltd, Registered Offices: 80 Strand, London WC2R ORL, England

puffinbooks.com

First published 2010
1

Text copyright © Chris Bradford, 2010
Cover illustration copyright © Paul Young, 2010
All rights reserved
The moral right of the author and illustrator has been asserted

Set in Bembo 11.5/15.75pt
Typeset by Palimpsest Book Production Limited, Grangemouth, Stirlingshire
Made and printed in England by Clays Ltd, St Ives plc

British Library Cataloguing in Publication Data
A CIP catalogue record for this book is available from the British Library

ISBN: 978-0-956-28777-9

Disclaimer: *Young Samurai: The Way of Fire* is a work of fiction, and while based on real historical
figures, events and locations, the book does not profess to be accurate in this regard. *Young Samurai:
The Way of Fire* is more an echo of the times than a re-enactment of history.

Warning: Do not attempt any of the techniques described within this book without the supervision of
a qualified martial arts instructor. These can be highly dangerous moves and result in fatal injuries. The
author and publisher take no responsibility for any injuries resulting from attempting these techniques.

www.greenpenguin.co.uk

Penguin Books is committed to a sustainable future
for our business, our readers and our planet.
The book in your hands is made from paper
certified by the Forest Stewardship Council.

CONTENTS

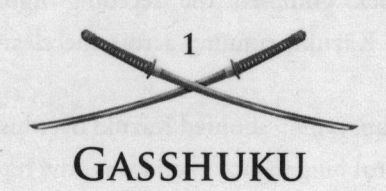

1

GASSHUKU

Koya-san, Japan, October 1612

'RUN!' bellowed Sensei Hosokawa, directing Jack over a fallen log in the forest.

Driven on by his swordmaster's command, Jack sprinted along the narrow log. His feet slid from under him and Jack flung out his arms in a desperate attempt to keep his balance.

Out of nowhere a thick shaft of bamboo swung straight at his head. Jack ducked, the rock-hard stem barely missing his skull. He stumbled on a few more paces and had almost reached the end of the log, when he was caught in the gut by a second bamboo cane. It sprang out of the forest, knocking him to the ground.

Reeling from the blow and spitting dirt, Jack struggled to all fours. His right hand grabbed at the log for support, then flared with pain as someone stamped on his fingers. He cried out. Through eyes screwed up in

1

agony, Jack glimpsed the receding figure of his archrival, Kazuki, running across the clearing ahead of him.

'Keep up, *gaijin*!' shouted Kazuki over his shoulder.

The throbbing in Jack's hand was now replaced by a burst of anger at seeing Kazuki's gloating face disappear among the tall cedar trees in the direction of the next training challenge.

A dark-haired Japanese girl dropped down beside Jack.

'Are you all right?' she asked, breathless from just having crossed the log herself. 'He didn't break your fingers, did he?'

'I'll be fine,' replied Jack through gritted teeth, looking into the face of his best friend Akiko.

'He did that on purpose!' she exclaimed, her pretty half-moon eyes narrowing in annoyance.

'Don't worry about it,' said Jack, having spotted Sensei Kyuzo, their *taijutsu* master, emerge from the forest. 'It looks like I've got worse problems than Kazuki.'

'Get up!' snarled Sensei Kyuzo, his beady eyes boring into Jack. The ill-tempered sensei was smaller than Jack, but as ferocious as an Akita fighting dog. He taught unarmed combat at the *Niten Ichi Ryū*, the samurai school in Kyoto that was governed by Jack's guardian, the legendary swordmaster Masamoto Takeshi.

Sensei Kyuzo briefly glanced at Akiko. 'What are

2

you waiting for? This is a *gasshuku*, not a tea ceremony. Keep moving!'

Akiko threw Jack an uneasy smile and ran on.

'So you're a monk for three days then?' mocked Sensei Kyuzo, glaring down at Jack as if the blond-haired, blue-eyed English boy was something vile he'd just trodden in.

'But I'm not training to be a monk,' Jack replied, getting to his feet and giving his teacher a bewildered look. 'I want to be a samurai warrior.'

Sensei Kyuzo shook his head with disgust. 'Ignorant foreigners!' he snorted. '"To be a monk for three days" means giving up at the first sign of difficulty. But I shouldn't be so surprised. I always knew that a *gaijin* like you wouldn't last long on a *gasshuku*.'

'I'm not giving up!' Jack countered, annoyed by his teacher's unfair harassment. 'How was I to know you'd spring bamboo traps on me?'

'*Zanshin*,' stated Sensei Kyuzo.

Jack stared blankly at his *taijutsu* master. He hadn't yet been taught about *zanshin* at the *Niten Ichi Ryū*.

Sensei Kyuzo rolled his eyes in irritation. '*Zanshin* is a warrior's awareness of their surroundings and the enemy. It should be instinctive. Give me twenty crescent kicks for failing such a basic training task!'

Several other students sprinted by while Jack carried out his punishment. Having already hiked up the

3

steep slopes of Mount Koya before dawn as a warm-up to the day's training, Jack soon felt the burn in the muscles of his legs. Every crescent kick was like fighting with feet made of stone.

The gruelling exercise caused Jack's breath to catch in his throat and he thought he was going to throw up. But since he hadn't been allowed to eat breakfast yet, Jack doubted he would vomit anything more than bile.

By his fifteenth kick, he was beginning to question his decision to volunteer so readily for the school's annual *gasshuku*. But Yamato, the second-born son of Masamoto, and one of Jack's few friends, had told him it was a privilege to attend the samurai training camp. Held in Koya-san, an ancient complex of Buddhist temples, the camp was located two days south of Kyoto in a secluded valley thick with forests and surrounded by the eight peaks of the Mount Koya range.

Yamato had suggested the intensive tuition would help them in their preparation for the selection trials for the Circle of Three later that year. This had been all the incentive Jack needed and he'd jumped at the chance.

Besides, since only fifteen students and three teachers were allowed to go, Jack had hoped that the *gasshuku* would give him a break from the bigoted instruction of Sensei Kyuzo and the bullying he'd been suffering at the hands of Kazuki and his gang.

But the *gasshuku* had proved to be no break at all.

It had been nothing but a regime of training, food, training, food, training and occasionally a little sleep. And he hadn't counted on *both* Sensei Kyuzo and Kazuki being there.

Once Jack had finished his kicks, Sensei Kyuzo dismissed him with a bored wave of his hand before returning to the forest to set more bamboo traps for unsuspecting students. Jack ran on as fast as his exhausted legs would carry him. He didn't want to be the final student to complete the test that morning, since the last was always given extra fitness training.

He followed the path that wound through the forest. The immense cedar trees on either side of him stretched so high they seemed to touch the clouds, their branches blocking out the early morning sun and leaving much of the path in shadow. Misty with morning dew, the forest was an eerie place to be alone and Jack was glad when he emerged into another clearing.

A group of students were gathering round Sensei Yamada, the third and final teacher to accompany them on the *gasshuku*. The ancient Zen philosophy master, with his long wispy grey beard floating in the breeze, was pointing to something on the ground beside a large stack of wood.

Jack spotted Yamato among the onlookers, recognizing him by his spiky hair. He joined his friend at the edge of the clearing and leant forward to get a

better look at what Sensei Yamada was talking to the students about. All Jack could see was an uninviting area of swamp.

A tall elegant girl with arrow-straight black hair exclaimed, 'Swim in that! Sensei, is this some sort of joke?'

The girl was Emi, the daughter of *daimyo* Takatomi, the Lord of Kyoto province and one of the most powerful men in Japan.

'I'm perfectly serious,' replied Sensei Yamada with a mischievous twinkle in his eyes.

Jack and the others inspected the noxious patch of oozing mud with dismay.

No one in their right mind would walk across it — let alone *swim* in it!

2

RIVER FIGHT

Huffing and puffing, a rotund boy with thick bushy eyebrows staggered across the clearing. It was Jack's friend Saburo.

'When are we going to have breakfast?' panted Saburo, wiping the sweat from his brow. 'I'm starving!'

Jack knew his friend hadn't wanted to come on the *gasshuku*, but the boy's elder brother had threatened to tell their father if he didn't go.

'As soon as you retrieve this rock from the bottom of the swamp,' explained Sensei Yamada, casting a large round stone into the murky depths.

It briefly floated alongside the rest of the surface scum before being swallowed up whole by the bog. Saburo glanced down at the revolting mud pit, then at all the reluctant students gathered along its edge.

'What's everyone waiting for then?' said Saburo, diving straight in.

Jack's full-figured friend belly-flopped on the surface,

7

sending clods of marshy mud flying everywhere. One hit Kazuki square in the face, causing a ripple of amusement among the class. Jack couldn't help but laugh loudest. Kazuki glared at him as the stinking sludge trickled down his nose.

'That's *karma* for stamping on your hand,' Akiko whispered, exchanging a knowing look with Jack.

They watched as Saburo sank slowly beneath the surface and emerged several moments later covered in slime, but brandishing the stone.

'See you at breakfast!' he cried, dragging himself out of the pit and running off to the *shukubo*, their temple lodgings in Koya-san.

The midday sun glinted off the fast-flowing waters of Koya-san's Tama River as the two young samurai adopted sword-fighting stances and sized one another up.

'I'm going to feed you to the fish, *gaijin*,' said Kazuki, pointing the tip of his *bokken* at Jack.

Jack raised his own wooden sword and prepared to defend himself. Kazuki had never liked him, for the simple reason he was a foreigner, a *gaijin*. Kazuki believed, like Sensei Kyuzo, that the Japanese were the superior race and that it was wrong to be teaching the secrets of the samurai to an outsider.

'I hope you can swim,' Jack retorted, trying to find a firm footing in the shallows of the river bed.

8

They couldn't have chosen a worse place to fight. Situated on a wide bend of the Tama River, the ground was carpeted with rocks. The stones closer to the middle of the river were rounded and slippery, while the ones by the bank were jagged and dangerous.

Jack had fought Kazuki before, but not in such challenging circumstances. One false move could mean a broken ankle or, even worse, a humiliating defeat for one of them. And Jack was determined it wasn't going to be him.

A blur of bright blue flashed across the river's surface as a kingfisher snatched a silvery fish from its waters. In that moment Kazuki struck, his blade arcing towards Jack's neck.

Jack was almost caught out, but instinctively blocked the attack. Deflecting it to one side, he retaliated with a lethal slice to the head. Kazuki ducked beneath the blade and thrust the tip of his own *bokken* at Jack's chest. Jack stumbled deeper into the river, barely keeping his balance on the submerged rocks.

Pressing forward, Kazuki cut across Jack's feet. Jack jumped the blade, simultaneously striking at Kazuki's wrist. Kazuki yowled in pain as the blow connected, forcing him to drop his *bokken*.

Jack didn't have time to enjoy his victory. He was too focused on landing. The river bed beneath his feet was a treacherous maze of rocks and potholes.

At the last second, spying two larger boulders, Jack thrust his feet sideways and managed to land, legs spread wide, above the fast-flowing waters. He let out a surprised laugh, amazed by his luck.

But Kazuki, incensed with pain, shoulder-barged Jack in the midriff. Jack lost his balance, toppling backwards with an unceremonious splash into the river. Retrieving his *bokken*, Kazuki leapt on to the two boulders and stood over Jack. He planted the tip of his sword on Jack's throat.

'I win, *gaijin*,' he gloated, forcing Jack's head beneath the surface.

Jack struggled for breath, spluttering as the icy river water rushed up his nose.

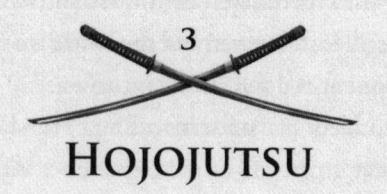

3

HOJOJUTSU

'*YAME!*' shouted Sensei Hosokawa from the river bank.

Kazuki reluctantly let Jack surface and made his way over to the rest of the students, many applauding his triumph in the sparring match.

Tugging thoughtfully at his tuft of a beard, Sensei Hosokawa, their teacher in *kenjutsu*, waited for Jack to emerge from the river and join them. Jack trudged over, his head hung in shame.

'Both of you demonstrated excellent samurai sword skills,' commented Sensei Hosokawa. 'Quick thinking saved your life, Kazuki-kun, and gave you victory.'

Kazuki savoured the praise, smirking at Jack who now stood dripping wet beside him.

'Though you were stupid to sacrifice your sword hand,' the sensei added grimly.

Kazuki's smile faded from his face.

'Jack-kun, your agility was exceptional – or else

you were very fortunate!' continued the swordmaster. 'But you still lost. Remember the battle isn't over until your opponent is down and *stays* down.'

Jack nodded his understanding. He should have known that from his bitter experience of the ninja Dragon Eye. The invincible assassin had killed his father and was now mercilessly hunting him down.

The ninja was after his father's *rutter*, a logbook that contained invaluable navigational information. 'A *rutter* for a pilot,' Jack's father had once explained, 'is the equivalent of a Bible for a priest. Until mariners can calculate longitude accurately, it's the single instrument we have to work out how far east or west a ship is. Such a logbook as this is the *only* way of ensuring safe passage across the world's oceans. You must *never* let it fall into the wrong hands, for whoever possesses it has the power to rule the seas.'

Jack had come to realize that Dragon Eye would *never* give up until the *rutter* was in his grasp, even if that meant killing him.

'Next – Yamato-kun and Hiroto-kun,' announced Sensei Hosokawa.

A thin wiry boy with a hard look in his eyes got to his feet and took his place at the edge of the river. Hiroto was one of the most vindictive members of Kazuki's gang. He had once beaten up Jack in an unfair

fight, so Jack now had his fingers crossed that Yamato would win this match.

It didn't take long. Looking to take Yamato off-guard, Hiroto attacked before Sensei Hosokawa called '*Hajime!*' But Hiroto had misjudged his step. His front foot slipped and wedged itself between two rocks.

Yamato, seizing the advantage, struck the power-less Hiroto across the stomach with the full length of his *bokken*. The boy doubled over and fell on his backside, where he floundered waist-deep in the icy waters. Yamato bowed respectfully to his defeated opponent, then carefully made his way back to the bank.

'Why are we training on a river bed, Sensei?' Akiko asked, as the students greeted Yamato's victory with a round of applause.

Sensei Hosokawa pointed to Yamato's wooden sandals. 'My own teacher once told me that if you are challenged to a sword fight, look at your opponent's sandals. If the wooden teeth on the soles are unevenly worn away, you can be sure your challenger will be off-balance and not much of a swordsman.'

With a sweep of the steel blade of his *katana*, he indicated the rocky river bed before them.

'Learning to fight on uneven ground will improve your balance. Remember, you won't always get a

choice of where to fight. As a samurai, you must be prepared for battle on any terrain.'

After lunch the students gathered in the meditation garden of the *shukubo* for a lesson in *hojojutsu*. Jack was intrigued. He had learnt many things since training in the Way of the Warrior, but he'd never imagined there was a martial art devoted to the techniques of rope restraint.

Sensei Kyuzo appeared, bearing several lengths of white cord. He indicated for the class to kneel and the students formed two neat rows on a flattened area of grass beside a small fishpond. In its waters swam an array of multicoloured *koi* carp that made the pond's surface shimmer like a moving rainbow.

'To control aggression without inflicting injury is the art of peace,' began Sensei Kyuzo. '*Hojojutsu* is the essence of this philosophy. The techniques that I'll demonstrate are useful for securing a saddle, tethering a horse and even hanging up your armour, but the art is primarily used for restraining a prisoner.'

He unwound one of the shorter lengths of cord.

'This is a *hayanawa*,' he explained. 'It's a short rope with a small loop on one end and is used for fast restraint. If you don't have one of these to hand, you can always use the *sageo* attached to your sword's *saya*.' Sensei Kyuzo indicated the braided cord hanging from

the wooden scabbard on his hip. He then beckoned his favourite student, Kazuki, to join him.

'There are four rules of *hojojutsu*. One, your prisoner mustn't be able to slip his bonds. Two, you shouldn't cause any physical injury. Three, never allow anyone else to see these techniques, otherwise they could work out ways to overcome them. Lastly, the result should always look neat and elegant.'

Jack tried to suppress a grin. It was so typically Japanese to demand that something as practical as tying up an enemy must still appear beautiful to the eye.

'First I'm going to demonstrate the diamond wrapping technique.'

Sensei Kyuzo doubled the rope and placed the halfway point at Kazuki's Adam's apple. He then wrapped the free ends round the boy's back, crossing one over the other, and wound Kazuki's upper arms tight to his sides. He brought the two ends together, before wrapping the cords round Kazuki's wrists behind his back and securing them with a couple of twists. A final tug pulled taut the whole diamond-shaped girdle.

Within a matter of seconds Kazuki had been bound and immobilized.

'He's trussed up like a pheasant ready for cooking,' whispered Saburo to Jack, stifling a giggle.

Kazuki must have heard them because he glared in

their direction, struggling against his bonds to free himself. But it was futile; the restraints didn't give at all.

Sensei Kyuzo released his protégé then handed out *hayanawa* among the class. Jack was partnered with Akiko. He took the rope and with several deft twists he had Akiko bound and unable to move. Jack glanced around. Everyone else was still struggling with the diamond technique.

'How did you do that so fast?' exclaimed Yamato, who had got no further than crossing the *hayanawa* behind Saburo's back.

Jack shrugged. 'Every day on-board ship I had to coil ropes, tie off sheets, reef sails and bind cargo to the decks. Even after a year in Japan, working with ropes still comes naturally.'

'Can you show me how you did it?' Yamato asked.

'After you've let me go!' reminded Akiko as Jack went to help Yamato.

Jack smiled apologetically then released her. The three of them gathered round Saburo. Taking the ends of the cord from Yamato, Jack slowly repeated the sequence of wraps. However, Saburo proved too big for the short length of *hayanawa*. The cord only just reached round his wrists, so Jack quickly tied off the diamond wrapping with a sailor's knot.

'*WHAT ARE YOU DOING?*' exclaimed Sensei Kyuzo.

Jack spun round to face the irate sensei.

'The rope wasn't long enough . . . to finish the technique,' spluttered Jack, 'so I tied it off.'

'Did you see *me* use any knots?'

'No, Sensei, but –'

'No buts!' interjected Sensei Kyuzo, pushing him aside and pulling out the knot.

'I don't mind, Sensei,' said Saburo quickly.

'You should do. Binding a person is a very serious matter. It's shameful for a samurai to be tied up. Some consider it worse than death. That's why we use wrappings, *never* knots!'

'But won't the prisoner escape?' asked Jack, shaking his head in despair. He could never keep up with all the strict social rules of living in Japan.

'Not if you wrap them properly,' snapped the sensei.

He grabbed Jack and spun him round. A moment later he had Jack's hands bound behind his back.

'If you think you're so clever, get out of that.'

'But, Sensei, he can still run away,' observed Saburo.

Snorting his disgust, Sensei Kyuzo knocked the back of Jack's knees, causing him to fall to the ground. Several quick rope turns later, Jack's legs were restrained too.

'*Now* he can't move, can he?'

'With respect, Sensei, I disagree,' Saburo insisted.

'What?' spat Sensei Kyuzo, enraged at the suggestion. 'He can still move his mouth.'

'I can't believe you said that to Sensei Kyuzo!' exclaimed Yamato over dinner that evening in the main hall of the *shukubo*.

They all sat cross-legged in rows as the monks served them their food.

'He was picking on Jack,' Saburo replied through a mouthful of *tempura*. 'So what if Jack tied me up with a knot? He didn't know it was dishonourable.'

'Thanks for your understanding,' said Jack, rubbing at the rope burns he'd sustained when Sensei Kyuzo had whipped off the cord in annoyance at Saburo's retort.

Jack reached for his chopsticks and gazed at the wonderful feast before them. It was their final night in Koya-san and this was their reward for getting to the end of the *gasshuku*. There was *tempura*, miso soup, sweet-and-sour seaweeds, wild potatoes and numerous other dishes Jack didn't recognize. Akiko had explained that this meal was called *shojin-ryori*. It was the traditional vegetarian food prepared by the Koya-san temples, the secret recipes having been passed down from monk to monk for over seven hundred years.

'Try the *goma tofu*. It's delicious,' Akiko suggested.

Jack used his chopsticks to pick up a soft pinkish

cube. He dipped it in the soy sauce before dropping the delicacy into his mouth. The *goma tofu* melted on Jack's tongue. It was deliciously rich, almost sweet with a strong sesame after-taste. He grinned at Akiko in appreciation.

'YOUNG SAMURAI!' proclaimed Sensei Hosokawa from the head table at the far end of the room. They all stopped eating. 'The last day of the *gasshuku* is always a time to celebrate. But tonight you must face one more challenge.'

There was a weary groan from the exhausted students. Sensei Hosokawa held up his hand for silence.

'Prepare yourselves for the Way of Fire.'

4

THE WAY OF FIRE

The fifteen students, led by Sensei Yamada, left the dining hall of the *shukubo*, crossed a curved wooden bridge and entered the forest.

It was now twilight and the last rays of the fading sun glimmered between the branches of the cedar trees. An eerie evening mist drifted through the undergrowth and the darkening forest took on a haunted air.

Jack's sense of unease only increased when he spied row upon row of moss-covered tombs. They lined the path on either side like giant bulbous mushrooms, the headstones seeming to stretch on and on into the depths of the woodland.

'Whose are those?' Jack whispered uneasily.

'We've entered the cemetery of Okunoin Temple,' Sensei Yamada replied under his breath. 'They are the graves of samurai warriors and lords who've died for Japan.'

'But there are thousands!'

Sensei Yamada simply nodded his head.

Jack glanced around. With so many lost souls in one place, he swore he could imagine the cries of battle echoing around him. Up ahead, a soft orange glow seeped through the mist.

'Is that the Way of Fire?' asked Jack.

'No, this is *Torodo*, the Hall of Lanterns,' explained Sensei Yamada as they emerged into a glade dominated by a large wooden temple. 'It is the holiest place in Koya-san.'

The four double doors set into the building were wide open, bathing the students in a fiery flood of light. Stepping inside, they gazed around in silent awe. The walls and ceiling of the temple were aglow with muted lanterns like the embers of a thousand dying suns. Not a single space was left unfilled by the strange brass lamps, their saffron-coloured flames combining with trails of incense smoke to create a magical, unearthly world.

Kneeling before a wooden effigy of the Buddha, monks in sand-coloured robes chanted softly, their murmur of prayer endlessly repeating.

'What *is* this place?' breathed Jack.

'This temple houses the tomb of Kobo Daishi, the great teacher of Buddhism,' Sensei Yamada explained, bowing his head to the main shrine. 'It is believed he is not dead but simply meditating, awaiting the arrival

of Miroku, our future Buddha. That is why there are so many samurai and *daimyo* buried here. They await his reawakening.'

'And the lanterns?'

'Upon each is engraved a name of the deceased. The sacred flames are kept alight to honour their memories. Some have been burning for over five hundred years.'

'Is *this* the Way of Fire then?' enquired Akiko, whose long dark hair glistened in the golden glow of the lanterns.

'No,' replied Sensei Yamada, picking up a lighted candle from a nearby shrine and leading them out through a side door.

The students exchanged confused looks and were even more baffled when Sensei Yamada brought them to the clearing with the swamp and wood pile. As they approached the marshy waters, Jack could see Emi raising her hand to protest against entering the swamp again. But Sensei Yamada stopped short and asked them to sit and put aside their wooden *bokken*.

'The Way of Fire is an ancient ritual of purification,' he began, holding the candle before him. 'It is a means of burning away attachments and evil, of letting go of the things that hinder you on the path to enlightenment.'

Sensei Yamada placed the palm of his hand immediately above the flame and began to chant:

'*Om gate gate paragate parasamgate bodhi svaha . . .*'

'What's he saying?' whispered Jack to Emi.

'It's the mantra from the Heart Sutra, the best known of the Buddhist scriptures,' Emi replied, watching with growing amazement as Sensei Yamada continued to hold his palm to the flame. 'It explains the fundamental emptiness of human existence.'

'Precisely,' interrupted Sensei Yamada, his hand remaining in place. 'The Heart Sutra teaches that "Form is emptiness. Emptiness is form. In emptiness there is no form nor feeling, nor perception, nor impulse, nor consciousness . . ." And so it follows, by emptying your mind, you empty your body of all sensation, all pain and all suffering.'

Sensei Yamada lifted his hand from the flame and displayed his uninjured palm for all to see.

'I trust that none of you've been neglecting your meditation practice while on this *gasshuku*?' he chided.

The students all shook their heads. Jack meditated regularly in the mornings now. He'd been introduced to the concept during Sensei Yamada's Zen class. And, though he'd been sceptical at first, he'd soon discovered it helped him focus for the day ahead.

'Good. Then I ask each of you to empty your minds and to hold out your hands.'

The students did as they were told, half closing their eyes and taking a deep breath to begin the meditation process. Sensei Yamada gave them a few moments then slowly worked his way down the line, holding the lighted candle beneath each of their outstretched hands.

When he came to Jack, he brought the flame so close the tip of it actually licked his skin. Jack, his mind calmed, was surprised to feel no more than a cool tingling sensation. Taken aback by the experience, he briefly lost his concentration and the heat rapidly rose. But before it did any damage, Sensei Yamada had moved on.

'Ow!' cried Saburo, sucking his palm where the flame had singed his flesh.

Sensei Yamada raised one eyebrow, but offered no sympathy. 'You clearly haven't been practising your meditation exercises,' he observed.

Sensei Yamada moved on to the final student, Kazuki, who was so confident in his own abilities that he lowered his hand into the flame itself.

'So have I passed the final test?' asked Kazuki, a smug grin on his face.

Sensei Yamada shook his head, the mischievous twinkle back in his eyes.

'This isn't the Way of Fire. This is merely a spark

before the blaze,' he said, tossing the burning candle on to the huge stack of wood behind him. '*That* is the Way of Fire.'

There was a sharp crackle and, a moment later, the enormous woodpile burst into flames. The air became filled with the spicy aroma of cedar resin and the acrid sting of wood smoke. The forest shimmered red, the blaze becoming so intense that the students were driven back by the heat.

'So who will be first?' shouted Sensei Yamada over the roar of the flames, indicating for one of them to enter the hellish furnace.

Everyone took a further step back. All bar Jack, who stood staring at the fire in disbelief. He had experienced some punishing tasks as part of his training to become a samurai warrior, but *this* was suicidal.

'Jack-kun,' said Sensei Yamada, smiling broadly. 'I would have expected nothing less of you.'

Jack, glancing over his shoulder, saw all the other students standing behind him in a line. He alone stood out in front, appearing to have stepped up to the challenge. 'But I didn't move . . .'

Sensei Yamada ignored the protest and beckoned him closer.

Jack had no choice. He couldn't back out now. He would lose face among his classmates. Kazuki, in particular, would delight in telling everyone at the *Niten*

Ichi Ryū how the *gaijin* had been too much of a coward to enter the Way of Fire.

Jack reluctantly approached the raging inferno, the intense heat scorching his skin.

A moth, drawn by the flames, fluttered in front of Jack's face before flying straight into the fire.

The little insect was snuffed out in an instant.

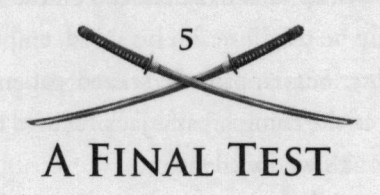

5

A FINAL TEST

'This is a matter of faith and entrusting your body to the fire,' explained Sensei Yamada, having completed the prescribed rituals.

The Zen master had sprinkled the ground with salt to consecrate the clearing. He'd then parted the bonfire with a long stick to create a flattened, flaming walkway. Finally he had blessed Jack, wafting the curling smoke around him and rubbing it into Jack's body.

Sensei Yamada gave a nod of his head to indicate all was ready and the students began to chant the Heart Sutra. Jack turned to face the final challenge.

He was still several paces away, but a scalding sheen of sweat prickled on his skin. His heart thumped within his chest, his mouth was dry with fear. The candle test may have proved the act of meditation could overcome physical heat, but *this* was no candle. It was a huge flaming pyre. He was going to be roasted alive.

27

Taking a deep breath, he choked on the smoky air. Desperately he tried to calm his mind, emptying it of all thoughts. Sensei Yamada waited patiently at the other end of the flaming path. Jack focused his eyes on the old monk's wrinkled face.

He stepped closer, passing through a patch of salt to purify his feet before entering the fire. The circling words of the students' mantra thrummed in his ears, while the crackle and pop of wood receded into the background.

Jack kept walking, his body cloaked in a swirl of flames, his eyes never leaving his sensei's face. He had no idea how far he'd gone as time seemed to melt away to nothing.

Suddenly Jack stumbled on a branch. He caught himself, but lost eye contact with Sensei Yamada. His concentration broken, Jack glanced down at his bare feet. The coals upon which he stood glowed a fierce red. He could now feel the blistering heat pressing all around him. His throat dried to dust and his lungs burned as he gasped in the scorching air. He thought he could smell the flesh searing on the soles of his feet, a sharp brilliant pain intensifying . . .

'JACK-KUN!' shouted Sensei Yamada above the roaring blaze.

Jack looked up, locking eyes with his sensei. He could feel the panic rising in his chest like a ball of

flame. The smell of smouldering hair filled his nostrils. He was going to burn to death.

'Focus on where you want to go, not on what you fear.'

His teacher's gaze was so intense that Jack felt his mind being drawn back to its meditative state. Jack fought his fear and grappled for control of his senses. With the help of Sensei Yamada, his mind quickly emptied of sensation and the fire lost its ferocity. Jack then resumed his steady pace through the furnace, the flames fanning him but not singeing his skin.

Exiting the blaze, Jack felt his feet come to rest upon a cool green mat of wet cedar branches. He breathed an immense sigh of relief.

He had walked the Way of Fire.

'Slow down!' pleaded Saburo, who hobbled several paces behind Jack, Akiko and Yamato as the class wound its way through the moonlit cemetery back to their *shukubo*.

Like true samurai, everyone had attempted the Way of Fire, but not all had made it unscathed. A few were suffering bad blisters on the soles of their feet.

'That'll teach you to forget your meditation exercises!' replied Yamato, shaking his head.

'I'm just glad it's the end of the *gasshuku*,' Saburo groaned, grimacing with each painful step.

'I don't think it's over yet,' Emi interrupted, glancing back over her shoulder. 'There's still tomorrow and I heard the sensei talking about one more final test.'

'But surely the Way of Fire was more than enough to prove our courage as samurai?' said Jack.

Akiko suddenly stopped in her tracks. 'Quiet! Something's not right,' she whispered, her eyes darting around the shadowy forest.

The students came to a halt. They could feel it too. There was an unsettling stillness to the trees. Not quite a calmness, more a deadness. The misty track they followed suddenly seemed haunted with the spirits of a thousand dead samurai.

'We *are* in a graveyard,' said Saburo, staggering on. 'No wonder it feels creepy.'

'We should go back to Sensei Yamada,' said Akiko, a note of urgency in her voice.

'But why? I can hardly walk,' complained Saburo.

'*That's* why,' said Akiko, pointing into the darkness.

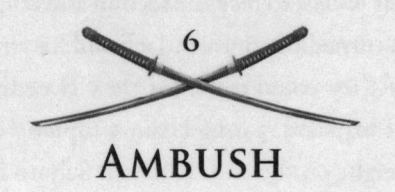

6

AMBUSH

From behind the moss-covered tombs, shadows were rising out of the mist.

The students huddled closer to one another, terrified by the nightmarish apparitions.

Suddenly three ninja, dressed head-to-toe in black hooded *shinobi shozoku*, sprang from the forest. They landed among the students, their weapons drawn.

Jack realized this couldn't be a random attack. The ninja had been waiting for them, which meant only one thing to Jack: Dragon Eye must have sent these assassins. His nemesis had somehow discovered he'd left Kyoto and the safety of the *Niten Ichi Ryū*. Beyond the protection of his guardian, Masamoto, Jack was an easier target. Now would be the perfect time to attack.

The young samurai scattered. The lead group sprinted off in the direction of the *shukubo*, but their way was blocked by the first ninja. Another group

drew their *bokken* to face the second assassin, while the last ninja turned to confront Jack and his friends.

Before they could reach for their swords, the ninja flung out his hand, a long chain whipping out with a heavy weight on the end. It struck Saburo in the gut, knocking him to the ground.

Yamato, his *bokken* now drawn, rushed forward to protect his injured friend. He sliced down at the ninja's head. The ninja, retracting his *manriki-gusari* with a flick of the wrist, spun its length round Yamato's wooden blade. Wrenching the sword from his grasp, he pulled Yamato off-balance and side-kicked him in the chest. It happened so fast Jack could only watch as his friend crumpled against a tombstone.

Akiko flung herself in front to defend Yamato, but the ninja ignored her and bore down on Emi instead. The *daimyo*'s daughter threw up her guard as the assassin blasted her with a devastating combination of punches and kicks. She managed to defend herself against the onslaught, retaliating with a desperate roundhouse to the head. But the ninja blocked it, capturing her leg with one hand and sweeping her to the ground.

As Emi rolled away between two gravestones, the ninja wound up his chain for the killing blow. He launched a weighted end at her. Without regard for his own safety, Jack jumped between them and cut

down with his *bokken*. The chain wrapped round the blade, causing the lethal weight to stop short of Emi's heart.

Before the ninja could whip the *bokken* out of his hands, Jack thrust it between the two graves, jamming the weapon into place. Caught off-guard by the move, the assassin struggled to untangle his chain. Jack seized the opportunity and launched a spinning hook kick at the ninja's head. Disorientated from the blow, the assassin stumbled into the mist-laden undergrowth and disappeared.

'Let's go!' urged Akiko.

She grabbed the winded Saburo and, with Yamato, hauled him up the path towards the safety of the Hall of Lanterns.

'Thank you,' Emi gasped, as Jack helped the *daimyo*'s daughter to her feet.

'Thank me when it's over,' said Jack, quickly unwinding the chain from his sword and discarding the heavy *manriki-gusari* into the bushes.

Jack and Emi hurried after their friends.

'Who are they? What do they want?' cried Emi, her face pale with shock.

'I think they're after —'

But Jack didn't finish his sentence. The ninja's *manriki-gusari* shot out of the darkness and wrapped itself round his throat. Letting out a strangled cry, he

was yanked off his feet and dragged into the depths of the graveyard.

Akiko, hearing his cry, ran back to save him.

Half choking to death, Jack saw her leap into the air, cartwheeling over his body to land a front kick in the ninja's chest. The assassin dropped his weapon as he was forced into close combat with Akiko.

Jack pulled the chain from his neck and staggered to his feet.

For a moment Akiko seemed to be overpowering her attacker, then the ninja thrust a spear-hand strike into a nerve-point beneath her shoulder. Akiko's entire left arm went slack and her eyes widened in panic. With her arm useless, she was unable to defend herself properly.

The ninja wound up to strike. Jack had only seconds to react. Recalling his time on-board ship throwing the mooring lines round dock bollards, he spun the ninja's chain above his head and released it. The chain sailed through the air, wrapping round the ninja and binding his arms to his side.

With the assassin immobilized, Jack knocked him to the ground and pulled free the *sageo* cord from his *saya*. With a few deft twists of the cord and a self-tightening gunner's knot, he had the ninja's wrists bound behind his back.

'That should hold him,' said Jack, running over to

Akiko who was rubbing her paralysed arm. 'Are you all right?'

'I'm fine. It's already loosening up.'

With Jack's attention focused on Akiko, the ninja silently flipped to his feet. Letting out all his breath and relaxing his muscles, he shrugged off the slackened *manriki-gusari*.

'Watch out!' Akiko cried.

Jack looked back over his shoulder. 'Don't worry. He can't do much harm with his hands tied behind his back.'

The ninja laughed. Jumping into the air, he brought his feet up and back through his arms. He landed neatly, his bound hands now in front. Jack and Akiko exchanged a look of amazement then, realizing the danger they were back in, sprinted away.

'Hurry!' shouted Akiko, catching up with the others. 'He's right behind us.'

'Not that way!' warned Yamato, as another ninja dropped from the trees to block their escape.

This assassin, a *tantō* blade glinting in one hand, headed directly for Jack. Through the slit in the ninja's hood, Jack could see a single emerald-green eye glaring at him. Jack's blood ran cold.

It was Dragon Eye.

7

DRAGON EYE

'Run, young samurai. *Run!*' hissed Dragon Eye.

No one moved.

'It's the *gaijin* I want,' he said, pointing the knife at Jack.

Emi glanced fearfully at Jack. He realized she thought this was a revenge attack for the time he'd stopped Dragon Eye assassinating her father, the *daimyo* of Kyoto, earlier that year. But Jack knew different. The ninja was here to find out where he'd hidden the precious *rutter*.

Dragon Eye took a step closer.

'*No!*' screamed Emi, kicking out to knock the *tantō* from his grasp.

Dragon Eye deftly evaded the attack, slashing her thigh with his knife. She screamed as she dropped to the ground, grasping her bleeding leg.

'Any other heroes?' enquired the ninja, placing the

tip of his blade under Emi's chin. 'It would be a shame to ruin such a pretty face.'

Jack knew there was only one way to save his friends.

'If you want me, come and get me,' Jack challenged, turning and running off into the forest.

He weaved between the gravestones, the undergrowth whipping at his legs as he went deeper and deeper into the darkness. Switching right, up a small rise, he then cut down a slope and dived behind a large lichen-covered tomb. His heart thudded in his chest and he could hear the blood rushing through his ears.

How had the ninja found him? Dragon Eye was like an evil shadow that never left his side.

Jack poked his head above the tombstone. The mist swirled between the graves, the tall cypress trees reaching up into the moonlit sky like the outstretched arms of the dead.

'Looking for me?' whispered a voice in his ear.

Jack spun round to be confronted by the deadly assassin. His single jade-green eye and the glint of a knife were all that could be seen in the encroaching darkness. Jack had only one choice. Clambering to his feet, he drew his sword and prepared to fight.

The ninja calmly put away his *tantō*, reached over his back and unsheathed a large *ninjatō*. The steel

sword caught the moonlight as he brought it in line with Jack's wooden *bokken*.

Jack didn't wait for Dragon Eye to attack. He knocked the *ninjatō* aside, thrusting his sword at his enemy's throat. The ninja's single eye flared in surprise at the speed of the strike. Twisting to one side, the tip barely missed his neck.

Dragon Eye retaliated at once, cutting his blade across Jack's gut. Jack managed to block the strike, but sacrificed a large chunk out of his wooden *bokken*. The ninja pressed forward with his attack, splinters flying everywhere with each blow Jack deflected.

Dragon Eye aimed for Jack's head. The razor-sharp sword sliced through the air. Jack ducked, holding his sword high to protect himself. The steel *ninjatō* cut straight through his *bokken*.

Jack stared at the useless stub of wood in his hand. How he wished he had the steel *katana* Masamoto had given him.

Dragon Eye gave a rough grunt of laughter.

Realizing his skills were no match for the ninja, Jack threw the broken hilt at the ninja and ran for his life.

He broke from the forest into a clearing, almost careering headlong into the swamp. Stumbling round its edge, he lost his sandals in the mud.

'You can't run forever, *gaijin*!' shouted Dragon Eye, hot on his heels.

Jack knew the ninja was right and stopped running. Taking a deep breath and calming his mind, he turned to face his enemy.

The ninja stopped too, his head cocked to one side, surprised to see that Jack had actually followed his command.

'So, finally you understand there can be no escape. Now where is the *rutter*?' he demanded, raising his sword and placing the tip to Jack's heart.

Jack didn't answer, but continued to focus on his enemy's face.

'Are you really prepared to die like your father over a mere book?' asked Dragon Eye, twisting the blade so it pinched Jack's skin.

'You should be asking whether *you're* prepared or not,' Jack replied steadily.

'What do you mean?' said the ninja just as the burning hot embers of the Way of Fire caused his straw sandals to burst into flame.

Jack had felt the hot coals as soon as he'd stepped upon the patch of blackened earth. He'd immediately stopped and cleared his mind in readiness for the heat. But Dragon Eye, so intent on pursuing him, hadn't given the ground a second look. The ninja howled in shock and pain as the flames licked up his legs.

Jack knew he only had moments before Dragon Eye recovered. Lashing out, he kicked the ninja as hard

as he could in the chest. Dragon Eye stumbled backwards, teetering on the edge of the swamp. Jack struck again, hitting the ninja with a double flying front kick.

Dragon Eye toppled into the marshy waters and disappeared beneath the surface. Jack didn't wait around. Knowing he would need help to capture the ninja, he fled back through the forest in search of his sensei.

But when he reached the cemetery, Jack discovered that his fellow students were still locked in combat with the three other ninja – and there were no sensei in sight. Picking up a discarded *bokken*, he joined in the fight, standing shoulder-to-shoulder with Yamato, Akiko and Saburo in a protective circle round the still-bleeding Emi.

Despite the students' combined strength, the ninja were proving too powerful for them and they were forced to retreat.

The lead ninja, his sword held high above his head, growled, 'Surrender or die!'

8

THE UNINVITED GUEST

The trainee samurai glanced nervously at one another. Even though they outnumbered their enemy, the three ninja possessed skills way beyond the students' training and abilities. Their only two options were dishonourable surrender or certain death.

'Never!' Kazuki shouted, sounding out a mighty battle cry. '*KIAAAAI!*'

All the young samurai, fired up by Kazuki's courage, brandished their own weapons and readied themselves for a fight to the death.

But instead of moving forward to attack, the three ninja looked at each other then simply nodded.

'Congratulations!' said the lead ninja, as they all pulled off their hoods. 'You've passed the final test.'

Standing before them were Sensei Hosokawa, Sensei Kyuzo and Sensei Yamada. The students stared open-mouthed at their teachers.

'This was a *training* exercise?' exclaimed Kazuki, his sword still primed to strike.

'Yes, the final test, and you showed true *bushido* spirit,' replied Sensei Hosokawa, a satisfied grin on his face as the students lowered their weapons with relief. 'Your courage is to be commended.'

The only sensei to appear displeased was Sensei Kyuzo. He stepped forward, his face screwed up with fury, and presented Jack with his bound wrists. 'Undo this demeaning knot, *right now!*'

Suppressing a grin, Jack hurriedly removed the gunner's knot.

'So who was impersonating the fourth ninja, Dragon Eye?' Jack asked, relieved to discover that the ninja attack had been faked.

Sensei Kyuzo scowled at him. 'What are you talking about?' he spat. 'There were only three of us.'

But before Jack could explain, Emi collapsed to the floor.

Sensei Yamada rushed over to examine her. 'She's been cut. Who did this?' he demanded, taking off his *obi* and wrapping it round her leg to stem the bleeding. 'No one had sharpened weapons.'

Jack stared at Akiko, whose eyes widened in a fearful realization.

'The fourth ninja was the *real* Dragon Eye,' she gasped.

Sensei Hosokawa and Sensei Kyuzo exchanged a troubled look.

Sensei Yamada continued to tend to Emi, gently parting her eyelids. She gazed blankly back at him.

'The cut's not deep and she hasn't lost enough blood to pass out,' he observed, 'so the blade must have been poisoned.'

'Can you identify the poison?' asked Sensei Hosokawa, his voice tense and strained. 'We can't have the daughter of the *daimyo* die on our watch.'

'We need the sword or the ninja to question,' the Zen master explained.

'Where's Dragon Eye now, Jack-kun?' demanded Sensei Hosokawa.

'I kicked him into the swamp,' Jack replied. 'But he used his knife on Emi.'

'Sensei Yamada, do all you can for Emi-chan,' ordered the swordmaster, ripping off his ninja disguise. 'Everyone else stay here. Sensei Kyuzo and I will go after the assassin.'

The two samurai sprinted off in the direction of the clearing.

Emi convulsed in Sensei Yamada's arms then coughed, white foam with black flecks appearing at her lips.

'I recognize these symptoms,' said Akiko, dropping down beside the trembling form of Emi. 'It's what the ninja call a Sleeper.'

43

'What's a Sleeper?' asked Jack.

'It's a poison that gradually paralyses the entire body until the victim suffocates,' Sensei Yamada explained, checking for Emi's pulse.

'Can you save her?' pleaded Jack. 'Surely there's a cure?'

Sensei Yamada shook his head sadly. 'Without knowing the actual plant or animal used to concoct the Sleeper, it's not possible to make an effective antidote. I can only ease her pain.'

'Wait! There *is* a cure,' said Akiko, her face suddenly brightening. 'The *haku-jo maru*. It's a flowering cactus whose blossom is said to counteract *any* poison.'

'True, but those cacti are extremely rare,' replied Sensei Yamada. 'They only grow at the top of volcanoes.'

'Mount Haku! It's not far from here,' Saburo interrupted. 'My father took us there last summer.'

'It's too dangerous,' replied the Zen master.

'But we *have* to try,' insisted Jack. 'Emi's dying because she tried to protect me.'

'I'll go with you,' Akiko said decisively. 'I know what the *haku-jo maru* looks like.'

'Count me in too,' Yamato volunteered, stepping up beside Jack. 'Saburo, you can guide us to Mount Haku.'

Saburo, his lip trembling at the prospect of climbing a live volcano, could only nod his head.

'No. I forbid it,' countermanded Sensei Yamada.

'Mount Haku recently erupted. I can't have you risking your lives too.'

'But you heard what Sensei Hosokawa said,' Jack argued. 'We cannot allow Emi to die. This is our only chance to save her.'

'But Sensei Hosokawa also said everyone was to stay here,' reminded Sensei Yamada.

'Isn't it our duty as samurai to serve and protect the *daimyo*'s daughter?' persisted Akiko.

'True . . .' agreed Sensei Yamada reluctantly, gazing at the unconscious Emi in his arms. Then a smile of pride spread across his wrinkled face. 'You *truly* are young samurai. Take the horses from the stables. But hurry, Emi-chan won't survive beyond a day. You must return by dusk tomorrow at the latest.'

9

MOUNT HAKU

Mount Haku rose from the earth like an enormous slumbering giant. Its steep forested shoulders led to a distant smoking peak, where a crown of snow glistened in the early morning light.

The four young samurai had ridden hard overnight to arrive at the base of the mountain for dawn. They skirted a large lake and tethered their horses to a tree at the edge of the forest.

'From here we have to walk,' explained Saburo without enthusiasm.

Jack was relieved to dismount the steed that he and Akiko had been riding. Having been a sailor, he wasn't used to travelling by horse. It was a samurai skill he had yet to master, so his legs were stiff and his backside bruised from the journey.

'We'd better get some water first,' Akiko suggested, taking a couple of hollowed-out gourds from their

packs and heading over to the lake's edge. 'It's going to be a hard climb.'

'Hey, look!' shouted Saburo, pointing to a large tunnel of black rock where a waterfall cascaded into the crystal-clear lake. 'It's an old lava tube.'

Jack peered into the pitch-black hole. It was like staring down the throat of a massive sea snake. The floor was slick and smooth from the flowing water while the ceiling hung with shark-toothed stalactites.

'My father said these tunnels form when a lava flow cools on the outside first. They start at the top of the mountain and can run for a long way, as much as a ten *ri*,' Saburo explained, cupping his hands beneath the cascade and taking a large gulp. 'I bet this water was once snow on Mount Haku's peak.'

'Come on! We haven't the time for this,' said Yamato impatiently. 'Emi could be dead by nightfall.'

They hurried after him into the forest. The trail wound its way up the steep slope and Jack soon found himself panting for breath. Saburo lagged even further behind, limping on his blistered feet, while Yamato forged ahead.

After an hour they reached a clearing and Akiko called for a short water break to allow Saburo to catch up. Jack had been thinking about Akiko's surprising knowledge of ninja poisons. Along with her mysterious

night-time disappearances at the *Niten Ichi Ryū* and the astounding climbing agility she'd shown during the maple-leaf viewing party, Akiko had once again demonstrated extraordinary insight into the assassins' world.

'How did you recognize Emi's symptoms?' he asked.

Akiko didn't reply immediately. Instead she looked sideways at Yamato who was checking the trail ahead. She anxiously bit her lip, clearly uncomfortable with revealing the truth.

'They were the same symptoms,' she whispered, 'that Yamato's older brother, Tenno, showed when he was killed by Dragon Eye three years ago.'

Jack now understood. Yamato was still greatly upset by Tenno's murder and he became angry at any mention of his brother's name.

'I saw the fight in the garden,' she explained, shuddering at the memory. 'Tenno couldn't stand. He couldn't see. Dragon Eye thrust a knife through his heart. A small mercy perhaps – better to die quickly rather than slowly by suffocation. Afterwards, when Masamoto carried Tenno into the house, I noticed the same white foam with the black spots trickle from his mouth. Later, when they bore him away for burial, his body had become stiff as a board. The priest explained to me that they were the symptoms of a Sleeper, and that Tenno would have died even without the knife piercing his heart.'

'Let's get going!' said Yamato, startling the two of them.

They glanced guiltily at one another, worried he'd overheard them. But Yamato was already disappearing up the trail.

Saburo limped past without looking up. He was clearly struggling from the relentless pace Yamato had set, but the resolved look on his face showed he was determined not to let anyone down, especially Emi.

They climbed for half the morning before the vegetation petered out into the black desolate landscape of old lava flows. If they thought the ascent through the forest had been hard, the dry grainy rock made the next stage seem almost impossible.

The uneven lava fields were difficult to hike across and the hot autumn sun was harsh upon their backs as they climbed higher and higher. Their pace slowed even further when they met with layers of volcanic ash. They had to trudge ankle-deep through cinders that scratched at their skin and feet. The billowing dust clawed at their throats and they were soon parched, their water supplies almost run dry.

There was little shade. The few trees that survived on the ridges of valleys carved out by previous eruptions were leafless, their trunks bleached white as

bone. Jack now understood why the *haku-jo maru* cactus was so rare. This was a graveyard for nature.

Reaching the crest of a ridge, Akiko spied an incongruous clump of green trees. They staggered over, collapsing beneath the welcoming shade.

'I can't go on,' said Saburo, gasping for breath in the thin mountain air. He inspected his feet where several of his blisters had burst.

'Don't worry,' Jack replied, passing the last dregs of water in his gourd to his friend. 'You've done more than enough guiding us to the volcano. You stay here and recover. We'll carry on.'

He gazed up at the snowy peak of Mount Haku, wafts of grey smoke steaming from its broken mouth. Their destination appeared distant and hostile, and Jack wondered if *any* of them would make it, let alone return with the antidote in time to save Emi.

'Over here!' cried Yamato.

Jack joined him further along the ridge and discovered the reason for the flourishing trees. A small stream flowed down the side of Mount Haku and disappeared into a large black hole.

'This is probably the start to that old lava tube,' said Yamato, dropping down to refill his gourd.

Refreshed by the water, the three of them resumed their climb. The ascent quickly became treacherous, their feet slipping from under them in the loose volcanic

ash. Still they struggled on, higher up the steepening incline.

Jack, pushing ahead, lost his footing and went tumbling down the mountainside. He collided with Yamato and Akiko, scattering them across the slope. As the dust settled, Yamato's scratched and bloodied face appeared; Akiko, not far behind, shook ash from her hair. Each wordlessly got to their feet, too tired to apologize or complain.

They reached the snowline, but the change in terrain didn't speed their progress. Having had no time to prepare properly for the arduous journey, they wore only sandals and the freezing snow quickly turned their feet to blocks of ice. Still they ploughed upwards, spurred on by the thought of Emi slowly suffocating.

Eventually the ground began to harden as the snowfield gave way to lumps of volcanic rock and scorched earth. The terrain became easier to traverse the nearer they got to the summit, but the thinning air made each step a supreme effort of will.

Jack began to notice sickly yellow patches mottling the blackened ground.

A noxious smell wafted through the air.

Then Yamato vomited, the contents of his stomach spewing out like a mini eruption.

10

THE FLAMING FLOWER

Yamato dropped to his knees and threw up again, now retching bile. With each breath in, he gagged.

'It's the fumes,' said Akiko, rushing forward to help him. 'He has to go back down.'

'I'll be fine!' spluttered Yamato as he struggled to his feet, tears streaming down his face in the acrid atmosphere.

'You *can't* go on,' insisted Akiko, gagging hard herself. 'Go back and wait with Saburo.'

Yamato tried to argue, but couldn't. Reluctantly he retreated down the slope. Mount Haku had defeated him.

'This is Hell!' wheezed Jack, his stomach turning over in the vile rotten-egg smell of the air.

He looked up at the steaming cracked peak of Mount Haku. Yellow and white traces of sulphur scarred the ground like a contagious skin disease. Shattered rocks littered the cracked earth through

which the mountain belched poisonous clouds of gas.

Nothing could possibly grow here.

Jack realized their quest was futile.

Akiko pulled a spare cotton *obi* from her pack. Ripping the belt in half, she passed Jack a length then wrapped her own section round her face. Jack did the same and the gut-wrenching fumes were partially blocked out.

She pointed up ahead. Through the smoke, Jack thought he could see the outline of a man-made structure. As they approached, he was amazed to discover a wooden shrine.

'*Who* would build a shrine on top of a live volcano?' said Jack.

'Mount Haku is one of Japan's three most sacred mountains,' explained Akiko. 'The local monks pray here and make offerings to appease the mountain god.'

'Did *we* bring an offering?' asked Jack.

She shook her head. 'But it would be worth us praying for a *haku-jo maru*.'

Akiko bowed two times before the shrine then clapped twice to awaken the spirits. She made her wish and bowed once in thanks.

They searched the alien landscape, but could see little through the swirling fumes, let alone anything that resembled a cactus. Akiko shrugged despondently and Jack kicked out hard at a nearby rock. They had failed. Emi was going to die. And it would be his fault.

The mountain rumbled. The ground shuddered and the air cleared briefly.

'I can see one!' shouted Akiko, pointing to the summit up ahead.

Jack felt his heart fill with hope as he too spied a small solitary cactus growing on the very lip of the volcano itself.

Then the mountain fell silent and the smoke closed in around them once more.

As they picked their way across the treacherous terrain towards the legendary plant, neither of them discussed the brief earth tremor. Akiko was clearly as afraid as Jack of what it might signify. Trying to ignore his growing fear, Jack focused on retrieving the precious cactus flower.

They reached the edge of the crater, a jagged line of emptiness that fell away as if the world had collapsed in on itself. Jack could see nothing in the abyss below, but the air was hot, stinking and barely breathable. He felt light-headed and sick and could see Akiko struggling to cope too. They skirted the crater towards the cactus until they could go no further.

Before them lay a stretch of old grey lava, its charred surface rippling like a stormy ocean, the crest of each wave sharp and spiny. On the other side was the cactus.

'It looks solid enough,' commented Akiko, picking up a loose rock and throwing it on to the lava.

The stone bounced a couple of times before coming to a rest. Reassured, Akiko then placed a foot on the rough, knife-edged surface.

'Be careful,' said Jack. Though the ground appeared firm, he was worried she might trip and fall only to be skewered on the hardened spikes of lava.

Akiko nodded her understanding and took a moment to plan her route. Unexpectedly she swayed and fell backwards. Jack caught her in his arms.

'I thought I was going to black out,' she gasped.

Jack offered her some water. 'It's the heat – and the air – we can hardly breathe. You should go back.'

'I'll be all right in a moment,' she said, pushing his hand away. 'It's Emi whose time is running out. I'm afraid it's down to you now.'

Exhausted and nauseous, Jack was in no state to attempt such a crossing, but he had no choice. They had come so far he couldn't give up now.

Jack left Akiko and took his first tentative step on to the fractured lava surface. The edges threatened to cut his feet and it was hard to maintain his balance. He tried to imagine he was walking over the rocky river bed of the Tama rather than a live volcano.

Halfway across, he began to feel dizzy. Despite the *obi* round his mouth, the poisonous sulphur fumes still seeped into his lungs. No doubt his mind playing

tricks on him, he began to imagine the old lava beneath his feet growing hot.

All of a sudden he tripped and tumbled towards a spike of rock just waiting to impale him. On reflex, Jack whipped out his *bokken* and thrust the wooden sword into the ground. The improvised walking stick gave him just enough support to regain his footing. Then the charred ground cracked and the *bokken* sank into the rock. A fiery glow came from the hole and a moment later the tip of his wooden sword burst into flame.

To his alarm, Jack realized he was walking across burning-hot molten lava.

He hadn't been imagining the heat after all. The closer he got to the *haku-jo maru* cactus, the more intense the temperature became. Jack began to panic. He could fall through the brittle crust at any moment, the lava burning his feet to a cinder!

This was the *real* Way of Fire.

Jack fought for control of his terrified mind. '*Focus on where you want to go, not on what you fear,*' Sensei Yamada had said.

He needed to focus, to clear all thoughts of pain. Feverishly chanting the Heart Sutra mantra, he concentrated on the *haku-jo maru* and boldly continued across the thinning lava crust.

The small bulbous cactus grew on a rocky outcrop.

It bore a single long trumpet-shaped blossom. The petals, a pale vanilla yellow, glowed faintly in the reflected light of the molten lava.

How can something so fragile survive in a place like this? thought Jack, focusing all his thoughts on the plant.

Finally he felt his feet reach the safety of solid ground. With the utmost care, Jack plucked the flower from the cactus.

At that very moment, the volcano erupted.

11

ERUPTION

There was a thunderous roar and the ground shook.

Jack fell to his knees, clinging on to the rocky out-crop for dear life. The lava field began to split apart, blood-red lines spidering out across its surface like veins. Jack fumbled for his gourd. Pulling off the stopper, he dropped the precious flower inside. Akiko was waving frantically for him to join her. Ignoring the danger, he scrambled to his feet and ran across the frac-tured lava, jumping between the most solid-looking parts before they sank into the magma.

He made it across just as another tremor rocked the mountain and he stumbled into Akiko's arms. They ran blindly through the smoke and fumes, heading down slope, past the shrine to the snowline. Both soon caught up with Yamato, who was making his way down as fast as he could, his face now filled with terror.

'Did you get it?' he cried.

Jack could only nod. Behind them a great plume of

smoke rose into the sky, blocking out the sun. They raced through the snowfield as the volcano awoke from its slumbers. An explosion detonated deep underground and the earth was rent apart. The snow to their right dropped away, a great hiss of scalding steam shooting from the gaping hole as lava poured forth.

Half running, half falling, the three of them fled down the mountainside. Reaching the old lava fields, they could now bound down in huge leaps, their impact cushioned by the thick layers of volcanic ash.

Mount Haku shook again, clots of magma bursting forth from its summit. As rocks rained down, fissures opened up around them and fresh streams of lava bled from the volcano's wounded sides.

Knocked off their feet, they rolled head over heels down the slope. An avalanche of debris and molten lava now chased them. It surged down the gulley they'd escaped into. Scrambling up its sides, they just managed to reach the crest before the flow engulfed them all.

But now they were trapped, cut off on either side by rivers of lava.

The three young samurai, numb with shock, gazed at the hellish landscape of smoke, ash and fire. Jack couldn't believe they had got this far and found the cactus, only to be stopped by a volcanic eruption. It was as if the mountain god was angry with them for stealing its flower.

'It's all over,' cried Akiko, wiping the grimy ash from her tear-stained face.

'There *must* be some way off this ridge,' insisted Jack, but, when he looked around, he realized the grim truth. They were stranded on an island in a sea of boiling lava.

'Over here!' came a faint cry.

On the opposite side of the gulley, beside a clump of green trees, Saburo stood waving his arms and jumping up and down in desperation.

'We're cut off!' shouted Yamato.

Saburo lowered his arms despondently.

'Can *you* still escape?' asked Jack.

'Yes,' said Saburo, nodding his head. 'The gulley's clear on this side.'

Jack looked at his friends. They knew what had to be done.

'I'll throw you the gourd,' he shouted. 'It has the flower in it. You must get it to Emi.'

'But what about you?' cried Saburo.

Jack didn't reply as he launched the gourd towards his friend. The answer was obvious.

12

LAVA RUN

'No!' said Saburo, as the gourd sailed through the air and landed safely in his arms. 'There has to be another way.'

'Go!' screamed Akiko. 'Before it's too late.'

The ground shook as Mount Haku spewed forth more fire and brimstone. There was a sharp crack and several trees fell into the stream of molten rock. They burst into flame on impact. The tip of one tree, though, landed on the opposite ridge, the whole trunk spanning the river of magma.

'Praise Buddha!' Saburo exclaimed. 'You can cross!'

'You first, Akiko,' insisted Jack, pushing her towards the makeshift bridge before she could protest. 'It'll be just like running the log during the *gasshuku*.'

'But without the bamboo traps!' she replied, flashing him a nervous smile. Weaving nimbly between the branches, Akiko was across in no time.

'Your turn, Yamato,' said Jack.

But Yamato didn't move and Jack could see the terror

building in his friend's eyes. While Yamato hadn't had a problem with the log in the forest, Jack knew his friend was afraid of heights. Once Yamato had almost plunged to his death using a tree-bridge similar to this to cross a gorge. Now he had the added danger of being boiled alive if he slipped.

'I'll be right behind you,' Jack promised, stepping on to the tree with him.

Yamato shuffled forward. The going was painfully slow and halfway across Jack could smell the sharp aroma of burning pinewood.

The bridge was on fire.

'Hurry!' shouted Akiko, frantically beckoning them on.

The tree began to crack and splinter. Jack urged the petrified Yamato to move faster. The trunk suddenly dropped lower over the molten river. Yamato stumbled, screaming as he landed among the scorched branches. Jack lunged forward and grabbed him round the waist. Hanging above the lava, the heat was so intense that all the hair on the backs of his arms was singed.

'Come on, we don't want to swim in that!' exclaimed Jack, dragging Yamato to his feet.

Just as the tree finally succumbed to the flames, the two of them tumbled on to the safety of solid ground.

'You took your time,' said Saburo, helping them to

their feet and handing Jack the gourd with the flower in it.

'I'm glad that's over,' Yamato gasped, his face pale and drawn.

But it wasn't.

The last explosion had diverted the lava round Saburo's ridge too and it was now racing towards them. Soon the land upon which they stood would be swallowed up by molten rock.

'What now?' said Akiko, a note of desperation in her voice.

'Looks like there's only one way off this mountain,' said Saburo.

He pointed to the entrance of the old lava tube. Miraculously, the meltwater stream was still running into it, though the flow was rapidly ebbing away.

'You *are* joking!' said Akiko, vigorously shaking her head.

'It's that or cremation,' replied Saburo. And, without a moment's hesitation, he launched himself into the hole, sliding away in the darkness.

'He's either crazy, or the bravest samurai I've ever met,' exclaimed Yamato. 'But what other choice do we have?'

Taking a brief glance around, he then jumped down the tube after Saburo.

Akiko looked at Jack, who was securing the gourd

into his *obi*. The lava was about to engulf them. Time was running out.

'If . . . if we don't make it . . . I want you to know I-I . . .' stammered Akiko, her eyes brimming with tears.

There was the sound of an almighty explosion from within the belly of the volcano.

'Go!' urged Jack.

Akiko pushed off down the tunnel, Jack following close behind.

He found himself quickly picking up speed as the incline steepened. The tunnel twisted and turned through terrifying blackness. All he could hear was the rush of wind and the gush of running water.

Something hard and brittle whipped into his face, shattering on impact. He felt the warm wetness of blood run down his cheek. Then he remembered the shark-toothed stalactites he'd seen at the lake and lay flat in the hope he would be lucky enough to avoid the razor-sharp shards of rock.

He could hear the cries of his friends ahead of him. The tunnel was becoming lighter. They must be nearing the end of this insane deathslide. Then he realized the orange glow was coming from *behind*. He glanced back to see a wall of red-hot lava coursing down the tube after him, the meltwater bursting into steam on contact.

Jack could do little but pray he'd outrun it.

13

ANTIDOTE

Jack shot out of the end of the tunnel like a cannonball and plunged down into the depths of the lake.

Despite the shock, he swam away underwater, kicking as hard as he could. Surfacing, he turned to see the fiery lava burst out the hole and pour into the lake. Huge clouds of steam billowed into the sky. The lava solidified, slowing and blocking the flow of magma from the lava tube.

A shock wave rolled across the lake, washing Jack and the others towards the shore. Bobbing in the water, they stared at each other utterly astonished to have survived.

'You're crazy, Saburo!' exclaimed Akiko, dunking Saburo's head beneath the lake's surface.

'Maybe,' he spluttered. 'But it did save us a long hike down.'

They all laughed with relief.

'But where's the flower?' asked Yamato urgently.

Jack smiled, holding up the precious gourd in his hand.

Yamato looked at the sun, hazy in the ash-cloaked sky. 'It's gone midday,' he said. 'We have to hurry. We still have a long ride ahead of us.'

By the time they reached Koya-san, the sun had set. They hadn't stopped to rest or eat and even their horses were near exhaustion as they struggled up Mount Koya to the temple valley. The four young samurai led their steeds to a water trough and ran the final stretch.

At the *shukubo*, Kazuki was the first to greet them. His eyes widened with amazement at the appearance of the four tattered, bleeding and scorched samurai. He said nothing, but there was an urgency to his stride as he accompanied them through the cemetery towards the Hall of Lanterns.

When they reached the glade, Jack could see the body of Emi laid out before the Buddha. Enshrined in a halo of candlelight, she was surrounded by praying monks, all chanting as one. Bending over her, Sensei Yamada was sombrely putting a flame to a new brass lamp.

We're too late! thought Jack. Despite all their efforts, they had failed to save the *daimyo*'s daughter.

Sensei Yamada turned to face them. 'Did you get the flower?' he asked, ignoring their injuries and ragged appearance.

Jack nodded.

'Give it to me.'

Jack numbly passed Sensei Yamada the gourd. His Zen master hurriedly emptied its contents into a brass bowl. The pale vanilla-yellow flower floated on the water's surface like a precious jewel.

'Can you still save Emi?' asked Akiko.

'Perhaps,' replied their sensei. 'The monks have been using the power of prayer to extend her life. But the poison's run deep. She's barely breathing.'

Working fast, Sensei Yamada pulled the petals from the stem. He immediately lay two over Emi's eyes. Crushing several others, he rubbed the flakes into her leg wound. Next he mixed broken bits of stem with a red resin, burning the resulting incense under her nose. Finally he boiled the remaining petals and with great care poured the liquid down her throat.

'Will that be enough?' asked Akiko.

'Only time will tell,' said Sensei Yamada, putting down the empty cup. 'But for a plant to survive on a volcano, it has to be completely resistant to poisoning. If anything can revive Emi, this will.'

The monks continued to chant.

Without a moment's hesitation, Jack knelt down and joined in the prayers, asking his own God for Emi's salvation. While ninja were the enemy of all

samurai, Jack knew *he* had been the reason for Dragon Eye's appearance. His nemesis had been after the *rutter*. But Jack couldn't reveal where it was. His father had sworn him to secrecy, warning him never to let it fall into the wrong hands. But that didn't wipe away the guilt Jack now felt.

Jack was still praying when the first light of dawn filtered through the forest.

Emi hadn't moved.

'You must sleep, Jack,' urged Akiko, bringing him some tea.

'How can I?' said Jack. 'I'm responsible for this.'

'No, you're not. Dragon Eye is the only one to blame. He was the one with the knife.'

'Did the sensei find him?' he asked, not taking his eyes off Emi.

'No. They followed his trail, but lost it as soon as they entered the Iga mountain range.'

Trembling with rage, Jack clenched his fists so hard his fingernails dug into his palms. Yet again Dragon Eye had escaped.

Just then, the two petals on Emi's eyelids fluttered in a breeze and fell to the floor. Bending down to pick them up, Jack noticed that the flames of the candles surrounding her remained perfectly still. There wasn't any breeze.

He stared at Emi. Her eyelids parted and she gazed dreamily back at him.

'Jack?' she croaked. 'I feel like I've slept for days . . .'

'You have,' Jack replied, too overjoyed to tell her any different.

'What happened to your face?' she asked.

Jack's hand absently touched the cut beneath his eye. 'Oh . . . nothing. I fell down a mountain, that's all.'

Then Sensei Yamada was by Emi's side and Akiko quietly led Jack away to allow their Zen master to tend the *daimyo*'s daughter. They emerged from the Hall of Lanterns and joined Yamato and Saburo, who were waiting anxiously on the steps for news.

'She's survived,' said Akiko.

'You've saved her, Jack!' exclaimed Yamato and he punched the air in delight.

'No, *we* saved her,' Jack corrected, smiling at his friends.

'That's right,' said Saburo, standing and raising his *bokken* in a salute. '*We* defeated Dragon Eye!'

'This time perhaps,' Akiko agreed gravely. She glanced back in the direction of Emi, who was being helped into a sitting position. 'Next time we might not be so lucky.'

Jack realized Akiko was right.

The only antidote to Dragon Eye was death.

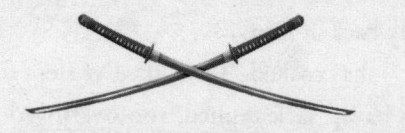

JAPANESE GLOSSARY

bokken	wooden training sword
bushido	the Way of the Warrior
daimyo	a Japanese lord
gaijin	outsider, foreigner (derogatory term)
gasshuku	training camp
goma tofu	sesame tofu
hajime	begin
haku-jo maru	rare flowering cactus
hayanawa	a short rope used for restraining prisoners
hojojutsu	the art of rope restraint
karma	fate
katana	samurai sword
kenjutsu	sword training; lit. 'the Art of the Sword'
kiai	a shout for focusing energy when executing a martial arts technique

manriki-gusari	a chain weapon with two steel-weights on the ends
ninja	Japanese assassin
ninjatō	the straight sword used by the ninja
obi	belt
ri	a traditional Japanese unit of distance, approx. 4 km
sageo	a cord used to secure the sword to the belt (*obi*)
samurai	Japanese warrior
saya	scabbard
sensei	teacher
shinobi shozoku	the clothing of a ninja
shojin-ryori	traditional vegetarian gourmet food prepared by monks
shukubo	temple lodging
taijutsu	unarmed combat; lit. 'the Art of the Body'
tantō	knife
tempura	deep-fried battered vegetables
yame	stop
zanshin	a state of total awareness; lit. 'remaining mind'

AUTHOR'S NOTE

I like to ensure there is a strong element of truth in my books – for instance, the *Niten Ichi Ryū* was a real samurai sword school. For the purposes of this story, though, I've brought Koya-san and Mount Haku closer together; in reality they're located on opposite sides of Japan. Mount Haku last erupted in 1659 and is how I've described, apart from its peak, which I've based on personal experience of climbing Mount Etna in Sicily. The Way of Fire is an actual ceremony performed by the Buddhist Shingon sect in Japan to mark the coming of spring. There are shamans in Hawaii who have been known to walk across hot lava. And lava tubes do exist . . .

This adventure occurs during the autumn of *Young Samurai: The Way of the Sword*. I hope you will read on and discover more about Jack's world of the samurai. Please visit *youngsamurai.com*

Sayonara!
Chris